FLOATING FACE DOWN

A Sheriff "Cowboy" Berkson Mystery Novel - III

Susan L. Pare'

www.susanlpare.com

TABLE OF CONTENT

MORE BOOKS BY THIS AUTHOR

Red

The House on Ludington Street

What's Behind the Screen Door?

The Mayor's Son

Willerton Woods

Cowtown

Let's Play Autopsy

A Bad Week in Hollister
A Sheriff "Cowboy" Berkson Mystery Novel – Book Two

Don't Smother Your Mother
A Sheriff "Cowboy" Berkson Mystery Novel – Book One

Crossing Sydney

Dedication

I dedicate this book to the following:
Jon
Bruce
Suzie
Nick
Joyce
M.C.
Don

Your encouragement keeps me going.

FLOATING
FACE DOWN

SUSAN L. PARE'

Prologue

Melissa Johnson stirred slightly; her sleep disturbed by a strange noise. She rolled over onto her back and listened. Hearing nothing more than crickets chirping outside, she closed her eyes and immediately drifted back to sleep.

Twenty minutes later she was dead.

He was glad he had worn his leather gloves. She'd put up a hell of a fight and her fingernails had left scratch marks all over them. He looked at the woman, who was laying half on and half off her bed, and knew he couldn't move her - knew he couldn't touch her again. He threw the pillow, which he had used to smother her, onto the floor. He felt a slight twinge of remorse. Then, he brushed the feeling aside. Now was not the time to get soft. He glanced around the bedroom, checking to be sure he hadn't left anything that could be used as evidence against him. He didn't worry about the rest of the house. After all, she was his mother and it wouldn't be unusual to find his fingerprints in her house.

He staged the back door to make it look like someone had broken in and then left. Within minutes, he was driving down the steep, winding road back to his small apartment in Hollister.

He wondered how long it would take the Sheriff's

Department to figure out that Tom had hired Hook to shoot his mother. Or, that Big John had been the one who actually killed her. I've planned it down to the last detail, he thought. Everything is in play. Now, it's just a matter of time and trusting that the Sheriff is smart enough to figure it all out.

Money truly is the root of all evil, he thought. A few months ago, I was just a boring guy living a boring life. Then, grandpa dies and mom is suddenly rich. Perhaps, if she had been willing to spread the wealth . . . I don't know. Maybe, I would have been happy with just a small part of what she got. Maybe not. It doesn't really matter now. The hard part is over.

My god, he thought, as the realization of what he'd done started to set in. I did it. I actually murdered my mother and framed my brothers for her death. All I have to do now is stay cool and, if all goes as planned, I'll be a millionaire by Christmas.

He smiled, as he thought about how he would spend all that money, and the life he would have. Women will be flocking to my door, he thought. I'll have any woman I want.

And, the cost? He heaved a deep sigh, as he realized that, without a doubt, the cost would be his soul.

Bobby Johnson parked his truck in an assigned

parking spot at his apartment complex and turned off the engine. He put his head in his hands and wept.

Chapter One

Bobby Johnson was drunk. When his boat hit the dock in front of Belle's Waterfront Café, going forty-five miles an hour, he was thrown out of his seat and landed head first in the water. He surfaced, shook his hair out of his eyes, and yelled, "What the fuck was that?" to the person who had been driving the boat.

Cal Cuddihey didn't answer.

Bobby swam the few feet to shore and laid there, his head on the sand and his feet in the water. He glanced over and saw Cal lying face down on the dock, blood pouring out of the side of his neck. As Bobby started to get up, a man knelt down by his side, instructed him not to move, and told him that help was on its way.

"I've got to help Cal," Bobby cried. "He's hurt."

"So are you, mister," the man replied. "And, it looks bad."

Bobby made one more attempt to get up before his alcohol-soaked brain finally registered that he was in horrific pain. He let out a wail that didn't sound human and passed out.

Sheriff Jason "Cowboy" Berkson was looking at Bobby, hoping to see some sign of life. He smiled when he saw Bobby take a deep breath. Looks like he's still alive and breathing, the sheriff thought.

"Bobby, can you hear me?" he asked.

No response.

Berkson looked over at Doctor Wasserstein, who shrugged. "He's sleeping it off. He had a pretty good snootful when the paramedics brought him in."

"Are you telling me that he's drunk?" asked the Sheriff.

"He was when they brought him in," answered the doctor. "Of course, the fact that we doped him up a little makes it all the worse. We had to put his leg back together, so he's fresh out of surgery."

"Isn't giving an anesthetic to someone who has been drinking a little dangerous?" asked the Sheriff.

"I guess we could have waited until he sobered up. It might have been a little risky to have operated so soon. It was a toss-up. Heads - yes. Tails – no. It came up heads, so we decided to go for it. He's still alive, so it looks like it worked out okay."

"What the hell, Doc? You think this is funny?"

"Kinda."

When the doctor saw the confused look on the Sheriff's face, he laughed.

"I'm kidding. Seriously, Sheriff, we knew what we

5

were doing. He'll be fine when he finally wakes up. Probably have one hell of a headache, though," the doctor said.

"I can hear you."

"Well, look at that. Our patient is awake. How are you feeling, Bobby?" asked Dr. Wasserstein.

"I'm not feeling anybody," Bobby slurred.

"How do you feel?" the doctor asked again.

"I don't feel good. There's something in my nose. I need a tissue."

"You're getting oxygen through your nose. You're in the hospital. You had a bad accident with the boat," the doctor told him.

Bobby closed his eyes, still not fully understanding what had happened.

"Bobby? You still with us?" the doctor asked.

Bobby slowly opened his eyes and looked at the doctor. "I remember," he said. "The boat hit something. A dock. We smashed into a dock. Where's Cal? Is he okay?"

"He's gonna be fine. He's still in recovery. A paramedic, who was having brunch in the restaurant, saw your boat crash and ran out to help. He probably saved your friend's life."

"There was so much blood gushing out of his neck," said Bobby. "My head is killing me, Doc. Can't you give me something?"

"What the hell were you thinking, Bobby? You know better than to drink and then get behind the wheel of a boat. Especially, that big ass boat," said the Sheriff.

"Hell, I wasn't driving the boat," said Bobby. "Cal was."

"That is your boat, isn't it?" asked the Sheriff.

"It is. But I don't drink and drive. You know that, Sheriff. Cal was the designated driver. Fuck, my head really hurts, Doc. Did I hit my head?"

"You have what is known as a hangover. Not much we can do for that right now. As soon as most of the alcohol is out of your system, we'll give you something stronger for your leg pain."

"No, it's my head that hurts. There's nothing wrong with my leg."

Dr. Wasserstein smiled. "Well, I can tell you, in a little while, that leg is going to hurt like hell."

Bobby raised his head slightly and saw that his leg was in a cast and elevated in a sling. "That's seriously one hell of a big cast. Did I break my leg?"

"Oh, yes," said Dr. Wasserstein. "You certainly did. You broke the bone between your knee and ankle. It's a big one. You're gonna need therapy once that leg heals. You can plan on being on crutches for quite a while," said the doctor.

"For how long?" Bobby asked.

"I just said for a long time. Probably a few months or more. The bone was sticking out a little, so we had to screw the pieces together and put it back in place."

"You screwed my leg together? I had to have surgery?" Bobby whined.

"You sure did. Dr. Messenly did a fine job, too."

"Dr. who?"

"No, not who. Dr. Messenly."

"What?" asked Bobby, totally confused.

"Doc," said Sheriff Berkson. "You okay?"

"Sorry, Bobby. Just messing with you. Dr. Messenly is the orthopedic surgeon who did your surgery. He'll be in to see you in a little while," said Wasserstein. "I have rounds to make but I'll be back later. Try to get some rest."

Sheriff Berkson gave the doctor a questioning look. "You been popping some of your own pills today, Doc?" he asked.

Dr. Wasserstein laughed. "Today is a good day. Guess I'm just in a good mood. We have two patients who are alive that could have died today. So, no, Sheriff. No pills. Just having a good day."

"Right. I guess that does make it a good day. I'm

leaving, too. See you later, Bobby," said the Sheriff.

As Sheriff Berkson and Dr. Wasserstein turned to walk out of the room, Bobby asked, "By the way, how's Katie doing?"

"Who?" the Doctor and Sheriff asked in unison.

"Katie. Katie Cuddihey. Cal's wife. She was in the boat with us."

Within seconds, Sheriff Berkson was on his phone calling the Fire, Water, and Rescue Crews, telling them to get back to the scene of the boat crash at Belle's Waterfront Café. ASAP!

Chapter Two

Every volunteer of Hollister's Fire Department was standing in front of Belle's Waterfront Café. Fire Chief Whitman was organizing a search party to walk the shoreline. Three of the volunteers, who had scuba diving certification, were already in the water, searching for the body of Katie Cuddihey

When Cal Cuddihey had crashed into the dock, he was thrown out of the boat headfirst. When he landed face down, a large splinter of wood sticking up out of the dock, impaled his neck. Bobby Johnson had gone over the side of the boat and landed a few feet from the shoreline. Katie Cuddihey, unfortunately, had been knocked unconscious by the impact and thrown backwards out of the boat into deeper water. During the confusion of trying to save Bobby and Cal, no one noticed Katie as the current swept her downstream.

Sheriff Berkson parked his squad car behind one of Hollister's fire trucks and exited his vehicle. He stretched his six-foot frame to get rid of the kinks in his back and let out a deep sigh. Days like this always got him down and he felt a lot older than his forty-six years. He'd been on the job for almost twenty-five years, but he never got used to dealing with death, especially the drowning victims. There was something about the color of a body that had been submerged in the water that made his stomach churn. Hopefully, they would find Katie Cuddihey before she turned that horrible pasty gray color and the fish had a chance to feed off her corpse.

He turned, as he heard a car approach and come to a screeching halt. Officer Simon Funtelli waved as he jumped out of his squad car. "Got here as fast as I could. What's happening?" he yelled, as he walked towards the Sheriff,

"Katie Cuddihey was in Bobby Johnson's boat when it crashed. We just found out about it. Chief Whitman is putting together a search team."

"Cal's wife? Shit. She was a nice lady. Why is it we always lose the nice ones?"

"Seems to be the case," replied the Sheriff.

"What can I do?"

"I'm not sure. I'll check with the Chief and see where he needs us."

"I heard Bobby Johnson was drunk when he plowed his boat into the dock. That true?"

"He wasn't driving. Cal was."

"Really. Was Cal drunk?" Funtelli asked.

"No. He might have had a beer or two, but his

alcohol level was basically nothing. The doctors are running more tests on him. They think he might have had a seizure, which caused him to lose control of the boat."

"He's epileptic? I didn't know that."

"No history of it, but you never know. We'll find out more when they get the test results. This may sound terrible, but I hope they do find something wrong with him."

"Why's that?"

"So, we can just call this a really bad accident, and put it to rest."

"How bad is the boat?" Funtelli asked.

"Pretty bad. I'd say it's scrap."

"Your phone is ringing, Sheriff."

"Seriously, Funtelli? You think I'm deaf or something?"

Sheriff Berkson walked out of Funtelli's hearing range and answered his phone. "What is it, Tim?" he asked.

"Tell the Rescue Squad to call off the search. Katie's been found," Officer Tim Carlson informed the Sheriff.

"Is she alive?" Berkson questioned, excitedly.

"Sorry, Sheriff. She's dead."

"Shit," said Berkson, and kicked the rear end of a red pickup truck that was parked next to him. "Where is she?"

"At Jake's Shop," Carlson told him.

"Jake's Bait Shop?"

"Yep. It seems Myrtle saw something floating out in the water, went out in her boat to see what it was, found Katie, and pulled her in."

Sheriff Berkson held the phone out and looked at it, seriously considering if he had heard correctly or if he was going crazy.

"Sheriff, you there?" asked Carlson.

"You're kidding me, right?"

"Nope. Myrtle found her in exactly the same spot she found Sylvia Toppers a while back."

"Who called you?"

"Jake. He said to tell you not to worry. Myrtle's guarding the body until you get there."

"Call Jake back and tell him I'm on my way." Berkson ended the call and walked over to where Officer Funtelli was standing.

"You okay, Sheriff?" Funtelli asked, seeing the disturbed look on Berkson's face.

"It's bad."

"What's that, Sheriff?"

13

"Katie Cuddihey has been found."

"That's good news, isn't it?" asked Funtelli.

"She's dead."

"Oh, I'm sorry to hear that," said Funtelli.

"Myrtle just fished her out of the water. We need to get over there right now."

Officer Funtelli looked at the Sheriff like he was nuts. "No way,"

"Way," the Sheriff responded.

"Myrtle. Like in Myrtle and Jake from the bait shop? That Myrtle? Please, tell me it's a different Myrtle."

"You got it right the first time. I need you to head over there. I'm going to go tell Chief Whitman to call off the search. I'll be right behind you."

"I'll go tell Whitman. I think it's better if you head over to Jake's before me. You know, with you being the sheriff and all."

"Nice try, Funtelli. Get your ass in your car and get going."

"But, Sheriff . . ."

"Now!"

"You don't have to yell. I'm going."

"Don't stop off anywhere, either," said the Sheriff.

"You mean you don't want me to stop and pick up

14

a dozen donuts to give 'em?" Funtelli asked the Sheriff, sarcastically.

"Don't be a smart ass," the Sheriff replied.

Officer Funtelli walked towards his car, turned, and looked back at the Sheriff. "I'll take the night shift for a month if you send someone else."

The Sheriff fought to hold back a laugh. "You're the best I've got to deal with Myrtle."

"Send Carlson. He's better and he's more experienced."

"Myrtle likes you the best. So, get your ass in the car and get over there."

"Two months. I'll do two months if you just . . ."

"I'm not dealing, Funtelli. Get going."

As he watched Officer Funtelli, slouched over with his head hanging down, walk to his squad car, Sheriff Berkson could hardly contain himself from laughing out loud. Funtelli slowly opened the car door, turned and gave the Sheriff a hangdog look, got in, and drove away.

The Sheriff stood there, a huge grin on his face, watching the car head towards the marina. Then, remembering the task at hand, the grin faded. He turned and headed over to give Fire Chief Robert Whitman and his men the bad news about Katie.

By the time Officer Funtelli stepped out of his squad car, he had decided to start looking for a job in a different town. Somewhere out west would be nice, he thought. He knew he was good at his job. He was as tough as they come. People seemed to like him, especially the women. He was the perfect example of tall, dark and handsome. Yet, for some reason, Sheriff Berkson constantly gave him the shit jobs. Like now, for instance. The Sheriff knew he hated being around Myrtle, yet instead of sending Carlson or some other cop, here he was again, dealing with that bat shit crazy old woman.

He glanced over at the bait shop and stopped dead in his tracks. Myrtle was sitting on an old folding metal chair holding a shotgun, while Jake stood by her side. The body of Katie Cuddihey, dressed only in the bottom of her bikini bathing suit, was lying on a blanket at Myrtle's feet.

"Hey, Jake," Funtelli yelled. "Hope that gun isn't loaded."

"It sure is," Jake yelled back.

"Myrtle, you want to put that gun down?" Funtelli yelled. "No need for it now."

"Well, lookie here, Jake. That nice sheriff sent me the handsome one."

16

"He sure did, Myrtle," Jake said.

Funtelli watched as Myrtle handed Jake the gun. He walked a few steps closer to them. "Jake, how about you break open the barrel and unload that gun?"

"Sure thing, Officer. Don't need it loaded now that you're here. Myrtle did a good job protecting that girl's body, didn't she?"

"She sure did."

"Didn't cover it up with no tarp either. No Siree Bob. We remembered from last time not to do that," Myrtle told Funtelli.

"You did real good, Myrtle," Funtelli said, and turned as a car drove up behind him. Doc Harris, the County Coroner, exited his car and walked over to where Funtelli was standing.

"Sheriff's on his way," he said to Funtelli. "I take it that's the Cuddihey woman lying there on that blanket."

"It sure is. She's all yours, Doc."

"This is weird, Funtelli. It's like .. ." He hesitated, searching for the right word. "It's like déjà vu."

"Tell me about it," replied Funtelli.

"God, I hate floaters," said Doc Harris, and walked over to take a look at Katie Cuddihey's body.

Chapter Three

Bobby shook his head in disbelief, as Dr. Wasserstein told him that Katie Cuddihey was dead.

"First you tell me that no one saw her in the water and now you tell me she's dead? I don't get it, Doc. How could that happen?"

"I'm sorry, Bobby. It seems Katie was unconscious when she was flung out the back of the boat. She couldn't yell for help, and no one saw her in the water. Everyone was busy trying to save Cal and you. She got swept up in the current and drowned."

"Have you told Cal yet? How is he, by the way?" Bobby asked.

"He's doing okay, health-wise. He'll probably be able to leave the hospital in a day or two. When he heard the news about his wife, though, he fell apart. It's to be expected. It's never easy to lose a loved one."

"I know how that is. Losing my mom took a lot out of me. I don't think I'll ever get over it."

"It was a double whammy for you. You have one brother who tried to kill her and another one who succeeded. I don't know how you managed to get through all that, Bobby. It was a lot to handle."

"We do what we need to do, Doc. I'm sure Cal will manage," said Bobby. "So, he's up and around already.

Good for him."

"Just trips to the bathroom for now. We'll see how he's doing tomorrow. He sure lucked out."

"He sure did," Bobby replied.

"Is there anything you need, Bobby?"

"Just to get the hell out of this hospital."

"Patience. We need to make sure that leg is healing properly before you leave."

"Ya? Well, I want to leave before I get some deadly infection from being in here."

"We're taking all the steps we can to make sure that doesn't happen," Dr. Wasserstein told him.

"I'm sure that's what all those people who died from sepsis thought, too. Seriously, Doc, I'm making arrangements to be taken care of at home. I talked to Charlie Hoppe - you know him, right? Anyway, he's setting up a room at my place where I can recover. I'll have a hospital bed, a private nurse, and later I'll get that physical therapist you said I'll need. If you let me know what supplies and stuff I'm gonna need when I get home, I'll make sure Charlie gets it."

"You've been busy," the doctor said.

"I admit I'm tired, but I don't want to spend one minute more here than I have to.

"Well, I want you here for a few more days, but I

don't see why you can't recover at home. That will be up to Dr. Messenly, though."

"Will you talk it over with him?" Bobby asked.

"I think it should come from you. He'll be in to check on you in the morning. You can talk to him then. I'll see you tomorrow. Get some rest now."

"Thanks, Doc," Bobby said. "I'll do that."

Bobby watched Dr. Wasserstein walk out of his room. As soon as he was sure that the doctor was out of earshot, Bobby picked up the phone and dialed an outside line.

"Charlie here," a man answered.

"It's Bobby. Cal's gonna make it. It looks like he's gonna be out of here in a day or two. But in any case, he's mobile and just down the hall from me. Get John Luke over here - like right now. Until I'm out of here, I want someone with me every minute. Tell Sammy, too. Charlie, I want round-the-clock protection. Got it?"

"You don't think he'll try anything in the hospital, do you?" Charlie asked.

"I think that bastard is just crazy enough that he would."

"Okay. I'll get John Luke over there right away. In the meantime, keep your fingers on that call button."

"Thanks, Charlie. Are you getting everything else taken care of, so I can get the hell out of here?"

"It will all be done tomorrow. Just relax. I'm taking care of everything."

"It's hard to relax when you know there's a person who wants to kill you a few feet away."

"Why not just tell the Sheriff what happened?"

"And, what? Be the asshole who takes away the only parent those little kids have left? I can't do that, Charlie. Katie would still be alive if it wasn't for me. I've done enough to hurt that family."

"What if he's not done? What if he tries it again?"

"If that happens, I'll deal with it. But, for right now, I'm not saying a word."

As he lay in his bed, Bobby thought back to when his affair with Katie started. What a mistake that had been. But, once he dipped his toe in the water, he wanted it to stay wet.

Katie Cuddihey had married Cal, one of Bobby's best friends, seven years ago. Bobby liked her well enough and enjoyed spending time with the couple. He watched as the Cuddihey family grew and was honored when Cal asked him to be his son's godfather.

A few months ago, Bobby had invited Cal, Katie,

21

and their two kids, Calli and Patrick, over for a cookout. It was especially hot in Hollister that day, and Bobby had suggested they bring their bathing suits if they wanted to go for a swim in his pool.

Immediately upon arriving at Bobby's home, the kids wanted to go swimming. While Bobby and Cal made themselves comfortable enjoying a beer by the pool, Katie and the kids changed into their bathing suits. The kids came running out of the house yelling "last one in is a thumb sucker" and cannonballed into the pool, getting the two men wet. Bobby jumped up laughing and reached for a towel lying on a chair behind him. As he turned to pick it up, he saw Katie walk out of his house, wearing a bright orange bikini, which left absolutely nothing to one's imagination.

Bobby felt a stirring in his groan and forced himself to look away. He had known Katie for years and never had any desire for her, but now he knew he had to have her. He watched as she sat on the edge of the pool and gently put her feet in the water. He couldn't believe that she had given birth to two kids. He didn't see any stretch marks and her breasts were absolutely fantastic. In his mind, her body was flawless.

He looked over at Cal, who was taking a swig of beer, and wondered how this man ever managed to get a woman like Katie. Bobby couldn't believe how jealous he was at that moment. He realized that he was getting excited, excused himself, and walked into his house to cool off.

Katie knew, Bobby thought. At that very moment, when she walked out of my house in that skimpy little suit, she knew how it affected me. She's as much to blame as I am for what happened. I just don't know how Cal found out. We were so careful not to get caught. Where the hell did we go wrong?

Bobby jumped as his eye caught a figure walking by the open door of his hospital room, bringing him back to reality. He reached for the buzzer and held on to it. He was tired, but was afraid to go to sleep. Where the hell is John Luke, he wondered.

Chapter Four

State law required an autopsy when death was not by natural causes. So, instead of Katie Cuddihey's body being transported to a funeral home, it had been delivered to the morgue. Doc Harris was set to perform her autopsy in the morning.

Sheriff Berkson drove to the Police Station, intending to do some paperwork before going home. As he walked into the building, Officer Tim Carlson told him, "Don't get comfortable. We've got a situation at the park."

"What situation?"

"It seems a raccoon has treed a couple of kids."

"Don't you mean a couple of kids have treed a raccoon?" the Sheriff asked.

"Nope. The caller said there were a couple of kids up in a tree and a big ass raccoon won't let them climb down. Should I call animal control?"

"We are animal control," said Sheriff Berkson. "Who else is here?"

"Besides you and me? No one. Herzberg just went home. Bell is on dinner break."

"Who's got the tranquilizer gun?" the Sheriff asked.

"Funtelli."

24

"Where is Funtelli, anyway?" asked the Sheriff.

"I haven't heard from him since he left Jake's."

"Get him on the horn. Tell him to get over to the park and help get those kids out of that tree. Get Bell over there, too. He's not doing anything. Tell them to be careful. That coon may be rabid."

"Oh, boy. Funtelli's going to love that. First, he had to deal with Myrtle and now a crazy raccoon."

"Not much difference between the two, as far as I can tell," the Sheriff said, laughing.

Officer Funtelli decided he wasn't answering the call. He needed some breathing room after dealing with Myrtle. Plus, he was totally pissed off at the Sheriff. He decided to call it quits for the day, put on some street clothes, and go get drunk.

Which is why, a couple of hours later, Simon Funtelli was sitting in Waxy's bar enjoying his second beer and starting to mellow out. Just as he started to take a long swallow of beer, a bullet whizzed by his head, shooting the bottle out of his hand. Funtelli, surprised by what had just happened, tumbled backwards off the stool and landed on the floor of the bar. As he started to pick his six-foot-six-inch body up off the floor, he heard three more shots ring out.

25

"Call 911," he yelled at the bartender. Tell them it's a 417 and to get here stat."

"You want them to bring a statue?"

"Just call them, tell them there's been a shooting, and an officer needs assistance."

"Aren't you a cop?" the bartender asked.

"I'm off duty. I don't have my gun with me. Will you just fucking call them?" Funtelli yelled.

"All right. I'm calling, already. Jeez, you don't have to yell."

Funtelli looked around the bar. Most of the customers were taking cover on the floor under the tables. He motioned to a few people, who were still sitting at tables, to get down. He started walking cautiously towards the back room of the bar. Just as he reached the door, a man came running towards him, waving a gun, and yelling for Funtelli to get the hell out of his way. Funtelli yelled, "No problem, man," and stepped back out of the doorway, giving the man room to exit.

When the man was a few feet past him, Funtelli reached out, grabbed the back of his shirt, and threw him against the wall, causing the gun to fall out of his hand. Funtelli picked up the gun, and, then, kicked the man in the ribs. "You owe me a beer, you piece of shit,"

Funtelli yelled at him.

He rolled the man over onto his stomach and looked around the bar. Customers, who had been hiding, were getting up off the floor and sitting back down at their tables. He motioned to an extremely heavy man to come over and join him.

"I'm a cop. I'm off duty and don't have my cuffs with me. I want you to sit on this guy until the police arrive," Funtelli told the man. "Don't let him move. Got it?"

"Got it," the man replied, and sat down on the shooter.

Funtelli walked to the back room, expecting to find gunshot victims. He scanned the room and saw two women and a man sitting at a table, looking guilty as sin.

"Are you guys okay?" he asked.

When no one answered, he repeated the question. They looked at him like he was speaking a foreign language.

"What the hell happened in here? Someone better talk right now," he yelled.

"We were just messing around," answered a young woman, obviously a little scared. "Billy's a little drunk and he went crazy. He does that sometimes. No one got

27

hurt, though."

"I almost got killed, you idiot. What the hell was he shooting at?" Funtelli shouted.

"That picture," the girl said, who was obviously as drunk as Billy. She started laughing, as she pointed at a picture hanging on the wall. "He said he didn't like that picture and he wanted to kill it. So, he took out his gun and shot it. That's funny, don'tcha think? Billy does the funniest things."

Funtelli shook his head in disgust and looked over at a picture of seven dogs playing poker. The picture hadn't been hit and was still in one piece. There was, however, a hole in the wall on the right side of the picture. Funtelli walked over to it and put his eye to the hole. He could see the area, in the bar, where he had been sitting, leaving no doubt that this was the shot that took out his beer and almost killed him.

There were also three holes in the wall on the left side of the picture. He looked through one of the holes and saw a sink. It was obviously in one of the restrooms, but he wasn't sure if it was the men's or women's. He was about to go check it out, when Officer Zeke Bell, gun drawn, entered the room.

"Are you okay, Funtelli?"

"I'm fine. The idiot on the floor out there is drunk

and took a few shots at that dog picture hanging over there. One of his shots almost killed me. The other three shots ended up in a restroom. I was just about to take a look."

"I'll go," Bell said. "Be right back."

Funtelli was about to take down the names of Billy's three friends and decided against it. He was off duty and it was up to Bell to do the paperwork. He heard Bell yell for him to 'get in here'. Funtelli walked the few feet to the restroom to see what he wanted.

"Whataya need, Bell?" he asked, and then noticed a woman lying on the floor. "Is she dead?"

"No, she lucked out. The bullet grazed the side of her head. If it had hit an inch or so to the right, she'd be dead. It's bleeding like a stuck pig, though. Get some towels from the bar, will ya?"

"I'm okay," said the woman, as she tried to get up off the floor.

"Ma'am, please don't try to get up," said Officer Bell. "We're gonna get you some help. Just stay where you are."

"I'm not staying on this filthy piss-stained floor one more minute. Help me up," she demanded.

Funtelli stepped into the restroom and took the woman's arm. "Get the other side, Bell. Let's get her outta here and into a chair. Did you come alone?"

"Naw. Carlson's here someplace," said Bell.

Funtelli and Bell helped the woman into a chair. Carlson walked over with some bar towels and handed one to the woman. He told her to press the towel against the wound and not to worry. The paramedics were on their way, he said.

Carlson thanked the man, who was still sitting on Billy, and told him that he could get up. He pulled out his cuffs, secured Billy's hands behind his back, and walked back over to where Funtelli and Bell were assisting the woman.

Still holding the towel against the side of her face, the woman reached up and pulled back her long blond hair. Funtelli stared at her. He felt like he had been gut-punched. My god, he thought, she's more beautiful than ever.

She raised her head, blood running slowly down her cheek, and smiled at him. "Hi, Simon. Long time, no see."

Chapter Five

Early Monday morning, Officer Simon Funtelli was standing in front of the Sheriff, staring at the floor. He was getting the worst chewing out he had ever received.

"You decided to do what?" Sheriff Berkson yelled. He had been screaming at Funtelli for the last five minutes and his face was getting redder by the minute. "Since when do you just decide to check out and leave before your shift is over? What do you have to say for yourself?"

"To tell you the truth . . ."

"Shut up, Simon. We had two kids in danger and the tranquilizer gun was in your squad car. You didn't answer your call. You ignored everything. Those kids could have been hurt bad. So, why the hell would you decide to go out drinking when you should have been on duty? You better have one good excuse. What could have been so important that you just up and leave?"

"May I speak, Sir?" Funtelli asked.

"What could you possibly have to say? Well, answer me," the Sheriff shouted.

"First, I didn't just leave work and start drinking. I went home first and changed clothes. Second, the squad car was parked out back. If someone needed the tranq gun all they had to do was open the trunk and take it.

31

Third, I told Herzberg that I was leaving a little early, so I actually did check out. I'm sorry I didn't answer the call, but after dealing with Myrtle for a couple of hours, I needed some time to myself."

"Well, boohoo. Little Funtelli had to deal with Myrtle. For your information, that's part of your job and you better learn to deal with it."

"It just seems a little strange that I'm the only one on the force that has to deal with her. It's never Carlson or any of the other guys."

"There's a reason for that, you know," the Sheriff said, starting to cool off a little. "She likes you and she relates to you. You're the only person I know that she acts a little normal with. That's why I always send you. You seem to think you're being punished. That's not the case. You're good at what you do, Simon. Stop being so sensitive and just consider it part of your job."

Funtelli smiled. "I guess I have felt like I was being punished for something. It's just that I always get the dirty jobs. Sorry about last night. Are those kids okay?"

"They're fine. We have one less raccoon to worry about. It went after Bell and he had to shoot it. That thing was huge."

"Was it rabid?"

"Probably. It's being checked out," replied the

Sheriff.

Funtelli glanced over at the cell where Billy was sleeping it off. "What are you going to do with Billy?" Funtelli asked.

"I'm charging him with public drunkenness, firing a gun in public, damaging property, disregard of human life, and accidentally shooting someone."

"He almost killed me, you know," Funtelli told the Sheriff.

"I heard about that. I could add attempted murder if you want."

"Naw. He's being charged with enough. Think he'll spend some time in jail?"

"Oh, I definitely think he'll spend some time in jail. What an idiot, trying to shoot a picture," replied the Sheriff.

"I like that picture. I sure can't figure out what pissed him off about it."

"To each his own, Simon. To each his own. Now, let's discuss your punishment."

"Do you think I could leave a little early today?" Funtelli asked.

Sheriff Berkson sat back in his chair and shook his head. "Are you friggin' kidding me?"

"Do you remember JoJo Kirkham?" Funtelli

asked.

The Sheriff looked confused. "What's going on with you, Simon?" he asked.

"JoJo. You remember her?" Funtelli asked again.

"Of course, I remember her. She was your girlfriend. In fact, I remember you said you were thinking about asking her to marry you. She disappeared a little over three years ago. What about her?"

"She was the woman who was shot last night," Funtelli answered. "She's back in town. I want to get off early so I can go see her."

The Sheriff sat back, put his feet up on his desk, and stared at Funtelli. "No shit?" he finally said, in disbelief.

"No shit," answered Funtelli.

"Do you know where she's staying?"

"She's at her parents' house. They picked her up at the hospital after she was treated for being shot."

"Well, I want to talk to her. There are a lot of unanswered questions about her disappearance."

"You telling me? I have a lot more than you do," said Funtelli.

"Hey, Casey," the Sheriff called to his deputy who was in the back room.

34

Deputy Casey George stuck his head out the door. "Whataya need?"

"I want you to go pick up JoJo Kirkham. Tell her I want to talk to her."

"Where is she?" Casey asked.

"At her parents' house. You know where that is?"

"I'll go get her," Funtelli interrupted.

"No, you won't," the Sheriff told him. "You're staying here.

"I know where it is," Casey told the Sheriff. "I'll be back in a few," he said and walked out of the building.

Officer Funtelli watched Casey leave, gave the Sheriff a dirty look, and sat down at his desk.

"I saw that," Berkson said.

"You could have let me go. You didn't need to send Casey," Funtelli told the Sheriff.

"You're suspended."

"What? You're suspending me?" Funtelli exclaimed. "What for?"

"You're suspended for two days, starting now. I want you to go home, get your act together, and come back on Wednesday."

"Why not just give me a two-day leave. I don't want a suspension showing up on my record."

Sheriff Berkson got up and walked over to the

coffee machine. He poured himself a cup of freshly brewed coffee and sat back down at his desk. He looked pensive, obviously thinking about Funtelli's request.

"You can have a two-day leave, starting now. Without pay. Now get out of here."

"Without pay? That's not fair," Funtelli whined.

"Screw fair. That's the deal. Take it or leave it."

Funtelli breathed out a deep sigh. "I guess I'll take it," he said. "Can I stick around until JoJo gets here?"

"No. You have one minute to get out of here before I change my mind."

"I'm going," replied Funtelli, and stood up.

"One more thing."

"What's that, Sheriff?"

"Before you leave, run across the street to Minnie's Diner and bring us back a dozen donuts. On you."

Sheriff Berkson sat back in his chair, thinking about Funtelli. A cop like Funtelli is a definite asset, he thought. He's smart and does good work. That wasn't so important a few years ago but things have changed here in Hollister. Up until a few years ago, the town was pretty laid back. We didn't need the smartest cops in the country. Sure, every so often we had to deal with a robbery or someone's home being broken into. Perhaps we dealt with a car being stolen or some drunk husband getting rough with his wife, but mostly it was just petty crimes.

Then, Melissa Johnson was smothered and since then it's been one big mess after another around here. Now, her sons, Big John and Tom, are sitting in jail while Bobby is living the good life with the money he inherited from his mother's estate.

A few months after that, Dr. Walter White, a prominent plastic surgeon from Branson, murdered Sylvia Toppers and threw her in Lake Taneycomo. And then, just to top it off, Big John Johnson's ex-girlfriend, Cynthia Hughes, commits suicide after she's arrested and is about to be tried as an accessory to Sylvia's murder.

Now, just last night, a woman who's been missing for over three years shows up, gets shot in a bathroom in a bar, and Funtelli is almost killed in the process.

I could have lost him last night, the Sheriff thought. Funtelli needs a little stroking now and then. I guess I better work on that or he might just up and leave.

Sheriff Berkson took another sip of his coffee. Yup, he thought, things are sure changing here in

37

Hollister, Missouri. And, I don't like it one damn bit.

The Sheriff glanced towards the front door as Deputy George walked in with JoJo Kirkham. He stood up, walked over to her, and hugged her. "Welcome home, JoJo."

He took a step back and took a long look at her. "You're just as pretty as ever."

She smiled at him. "And, you're even more handsome than I remember, Cowboy."

"Now," the Sheriff said, "how about we enjoy a cup of coffee and a donut, while you tell me where the hell you've been for the past three years."

Chapter Six

Bobby Johnson finally got some sleep. He woke up on Monday morning feeling like crap. His headache was gone but his leg was hurting like hell. He hit the button that dispensed the pain killer and waited for it to kick in.

John Luke had shown up around ten o'clock and, after a heated argument with the night nurse, was allowed to sit outside Bobby's room. At eight o'clock this morning, Sammy had relieved John Luke of his guard duties and John Luke had gone home to get some sleep.

Bobby started his morning by calling Charlie Hoppe to find out when the room for his recovery would be ready. He wanted out of the hospital – like right now. He knew the doctor would not release him until he could prove he would have everything necessary for his recovery at home.

Charlie told him the hospital bed was scheduled to arrive that afternoon. He had already hired two nurses who would work during the day. He was about to call a third one, to see if he would be available for the third shift.

"What do you mean, he?" Bobby inquired.

"It's a male nurse. What difference does it make? You'll be sleeping most of the time when he's working

39

anyway."

"I guess it's okay. What do the other two look like?"

"They look like women. They'll be taking care of you, Bobby. You're not dating them. I've checked their references and they come highly recommended."

"I'm gonna ask the doctor if I can get out of here today," Bobby said. "He hasn't been in to see me yet."

"It's still early. I'll call you later and let you know when the bed gets here."

"That's all you're waiting for, right?" Bobby asked.

"That's it, Pal . . . "

"What the fuck!" Bobby shouted.

"What's the matter," Charlie yelled.

Cal Cuddihey was standing in the doorway to Bobby's room. He raised his arm, made a fist, and then pointed his index finger. "Bang," he said loudly.

Sammy suddenly stood up, pushed Cuddihey out of the way, and blocked the entrance to Bobby's room.

"Hey, man," Cuddihey yelled. "Whataya think you're doing?"

"Get your ass back to your room," Sammy whispered. "Now, or they'll be wheeling you back."

"All right. I'm going. Just stay away from me," said Cuddihey. He turned, gave Bobby a dirty look, and

40

walked down the hall to his room.

"You okay?" Charlie asked Bobby.

"I'm okay. Get that bed now. I'm having an ambulance bring me home. I'm not staying one minute more in this place than I have to."

Bobby cut off the call and yelled, "Sammy, get in here."

"Whataya need?" Sammy asked as he walked into the room.

"Do you know why you're here?" Bobby asked.

"To keep people out of your room. Right?" he answered.

"No, that's not right. It's to keep Cal Cuddihey out of my room. If he had a gun, I'd be dead right now."

"Sorry."

"You've got to check every person coming down that hallway, Sammy. You've got to be sure that Cuddihey doesn't get close to me. Understand?"

"Got it."

"Doctors and nurses are okay. It's just Cuddihey that I'm worried about."

"Got it."

"Good. Let's not have anything like that happen again."

"I'm hungry. When do I get to eat?"

41

"You got a phone on you?"

"Of course," Sammy replied.

"Then order whatever you want and have it delivered."

"Here? At the hospital?"

"Yes, here."

"That's cool. Ya, I'll do that."

Bobby closed his eyes. His heart was beating way too fast, and he was shaking. He took a few deep breaths and tried to relax, while his body slowly returned to normal.

He hit the call button to summon a nurse and waited. When no one showed up, he hit it again and waited. He continued hitting it until a nurse finally came running into his room.

"Mr. Johnson, is that really necessary?" she said, as she took the call button out of his hand.

"I need to call an ambulance. How do I do that?" Bobby asked.

"You don't need an ambulance, Mr. Johnson. You're already in the hospital."

"Get me a friggin' phone number," Bobby yelled.

"I think you need a doctor. Just hold on a minute, while I get the doctor"

"I don't want a doctor. I want an ambulance. I'm

42

going home," he yelled at her.

"I'm sorry, Sir, but you can't leave until the doctor releases you."

"You wanna bet?"

"I'll see if your doctor is here," the nurse said and hurried out of Bobby's room.

Bobby was about to have a meltdown. For the first time, since he could remember, he was not in control. Again, he took some deep breaths, trying to settle down. He grabbed his cell phone and called Charlie.

"What now?" Charlie said as he answered his phone.

"Get an ambulance and a couple of paramedics over here. I don't care what it costs. I'm going home. Get it done, Charlie."

"I hear you, Boss. I'll take care of it."

Both Dr. Wasserstein and Dr. Messenly were trying to convince Bobby that he should stay in the hospital.

"I don't care about your rules," Bobby said. "Don't worry. I won't hold you responsible if I die."

"It's just too soon," Dr. Messenly said. "You're not ready to go home, yet."

"What are you gonna do for me here that can't be

43

done at my house?" Bobby asked.

"You need a lot more care . . ." Dr. Messenly stopped talking, as two paramedics rolled a gurney into Bobby's room. "I strongly advise against this, Bobby," he said.

"Noted. Now, get out of the way, please. These men have a job to do."

"Just stay one more day. You aren't well enough to leave," Dr. Messenly said.

"Thanks for getting here so fast," Bobby said to the two paramedics, ignoring the doctor. "I appreciate it."

"No problem, man," said one of the paramedics. "Nancy will be here in a few minutes."

"Who's Nancy?" asked Bobby.

"She's one of the nurses that will be taking care of you."

"Nurse Nancy," Bobby said and smiled. "That sounds cool."

Dr. Messenly stepped back and watched as the paramedics starting working. He looked over at Dr. Wasserstein and shook his head. "This isn't good, Philip," he told him.

"Not much we can do about it," Dr. Wasserstein replied. "Let's just make sure the transfer is done

44

correctly." He turned, as he heard someone walk into the room.

"Nancy Carson? You're the Nancy that's taking care of Bobby? I thought you retired," said Dr. Wasserstein.

"I did. And, now I'm un-retired. I just couldn't pass up this job. When this gig is over, I'm taking my whole family to Hawaii for a two-week vacation. And, maybe buy a new car."

"Well, at least I'll rest a little better, knowing that Bobby's in good hands," said Dr. Messenly.

Bobby glanced over at Nancy and grinned, leaving no doubt in anyone's mind, as to what he was thinking.

Chapter Seven

JoJo Kirkham's hair hid most of the bandage that was taped to the side of her face. She smiled at the Sheriff, as she sat down across from him.

"How's the head?" the Sheriff asked her.

"It's okay. It burns a little. The doctor said I'm going to have a scar, but I figure a little plastic surgery will take care of that."

"You're lucky that bullet didn't kill you."

"I don't believe in luck. It just wasn't my time yet."

"Well, believe it or not, I'm glad you're okay."

"Me, too."

"Tell me, JoJo. Where have you been for the past three years?"

"Would you believe me if I told you I was kidnapped and held against my will by a mountain man?"

Sheriff Berkson smiled. "No, JoJo, I wouldn't."

"How about I was taken by aliens and used for sexual experiments on a spaceship?"

"How about you just fill in the blanks, JoJo? Do you have any idea of the expense that was incurred trying to find you? Do you have any idea what you put Simon through? He just about went crazy worrying about you. He figured you were dead. After a while, we

46

all did."

"My parents knew where I was. They were the only ones. Well, there were a few others. But I swore them to secrecy and made them promise not to tell anyone."

"I'd like you to tell me where you were?"

"I knew Simon was going to ask me to marry him. I'm still not sure if I would have said yes or no. I loved him, you know. I just don't think I loved him enough to marry him. But, he's not the reason I left."

"Then, why'd you leave?"

"Have you ever heard of the McKenzie Experiment?"

"Can't say I have," replied Sheriff Berkson, wondering where this was headed.

"Of course not. Only a few people in the world know about it."

"What does that have to do with you disappearing?"

"Sheriff, I need you to promise me that you will never repeat what I'm about to tell you. Ever!"

"I guess I can do that. What about Simon?"

"He must never know."

"All right. I promise."

"Good. Otherwise, I couldn't tell you." JoJo hesitated for a few seconds, considering what she was

47

about to tell the Sheriff. "Three years ago, I was approached by some people who asked me if I would participate in a highly secretive program. It was only supposed to last a year, but the more the program revealed, the more my services were needed and the longer the program lasted. It's still going on. I can't tell you where I was taken, because I was sworn to secrecy. I can tell you that I was paid a lot – and I mean a lot – of money. I'm an extremely rich woman, Sheriff. I could buy this entire town if I wanted to. That's it. That's what happened."

Sheriff Berkson stared at her, as she told her story. "How often do you see your parents?

JoJo looked confused by the question. "I don't understand why you would ask me that."

"I just wondered if they're allowed to visit you at this secret place," he stated.

JoJo hesitated. "Of course," she finally said. "They bring Charlie to visit me."

"And, who is Charlie?"

"Well, my dog, of course. I can only see him for a little while and then he has to go back home. I wish I could keep him with me, but my work doesn't allow it."

"I see. Is there anything else you can tell me, JoJo?" he asked, already knowing that this conversation was useless.

"That's about it. Well, I can tell you that I'm glad to be back home, even if it's only for a few days."

"What are you going to tell Simon? He wants to see you, you know."

"I know. I'll tell him I'm sorry. I never meant to hurt him, but I'm engaged now. I'm sure he'll understand.

"Well, I'm not sure he will," said the Sheriff. "I think he needs some kind of an explanation. I don't think just saying I'm sorry is going to cut it."

"Then, that's his problem. Because that's all he's going to get from me," said JoJo.

"You've changed, JoJo."

"I guess being gone for three years, and going through what I have, would change anybody."

As she talked, Sheriff Berkson studied her face. He saw no sign of deception. She believes what she's telling me, he thought. "I'd like more of an explanation, JoJo. Isn't there anything you can tell me about these experiments?"

"Oh, no. That would be revealing highly confidential information. I'm sorry, but that's all I can tell you."

"Then, I guess we're done here. I'll have Officer

George drive you home. It was good to see you, JoJo. Take care of yourself," said the Sheriff.

"Is Simon here?" JoJo asked as she stood up.

"No. He's off for a few days. I expect he'll be lookin' to talk to you, though."

Officer Simon Funtelli stared at Mr. and Mrs. Kirkham. He was sitting in their living room, holding a cup of coffee, and listening. He did not interrupt them. He doubted he could have, even if he wanted to. He felt like he was having an out-of-body experience and was watching himself from across the room.

"We're sorry, Simon," Mr. Kirkham said. "We know what you went through, but we promised JoJo that we wouldn't tell you."

"So, she's only here for a few days?" Simon asked.

"Yes. We're taking her back on Saturday."

"I'd like to talk to her."

"That's not a good idea. Of course, she remembers you, but she thinks she's engaged to Dr. McKenzie. It might confuse her if you talked to her and brought up the past."

"I don't get it. What was she doing at Waxy's? If she's so bad off, why was she out partying?

Mrs. Kirkham gave her husband an accusing look.

50

"I had to go to the store," she said. "My husband was supposed to watch her, but he got so involved in watching some sporting event on TV, he didn't see her leave the house. We thought she was in bed. We didn't even know she was gone until we got the call from the hospital that she was there. I just thank the good Lord that bullet didn't kill her."

"You said she's over at the Police Station right now. If you don't think I should talk to her about the past, how is talking to Sheriff Berkson a good idea?"

"When Officer George came to pick her up, we figured it was easier to let her go than to get into all of this. She was excited that she was going to see the Sheriff. We were going to call him and warn him of her condition, but then you showed up. I'll give him a call as soon as you leave," Mr. Kirkham said.

"Perhaps, you should call him now. I know that this has been hard on you, but it was hard on me, too. I just wish you would have trusted me enough to tell me that she was in an institution all these years. I thought she was dead."

"In a sense she is. We lost our real JoJo three years ago. I'm sorry for you, too, Simon," said Mrs. Kirkham. "I know how hard her disappearing was on you, but we promised everyone involved not to tell."

Funtelli stood and shook their hands. "I guess I should be grateful that I finally know the truth. But, it's too little, too late," he said and walked out of their house.

An hour later, Sheriff Berkson and Officer Funtelli were sitting at a table in Minnie's Diner, drinking coffee. The Sheriff was listening to Funtelli, and shaking his head in disbelief.

"Are you serious?" the Sheriff asked.

"I thought Mr. Kirkham called and told you what had happened."

"He did call. All he said was that JoJo had a nervous breakdown and attempted suicide. He told me they had no choice but to institutionalize her in a facility in Kansas City."

"That's the other thing," Funtelli said, raising his voice. "She was only two hundred miles away. I can't believe that for the past three years she was so close. Plus, she never tried to commit suicide. That's a lie. There's a lot more to it than what they told you."

"What's that?"

"I knew JoJo was acting different. It probably started a few months before this all happened. She seemed upset a lot of the time and was stressed out. She was working more hours and constantly complained that her boss was on her case. I just figured the job was getting to her. We talked about her quitting and finding a better job." Funtelli took a sip of his coffee. He looked away, wondering how to put what he had to say into words.

"And?" the Sheriff prompted.

"She tried to kill her boss," Funtelli finally blurted out.

"She did what?" Berkson said.

"I didn't know about that until today, Sheriff. I swear to God. I last saw her on a Wednesday and on the following Friday she was gone. Her parents told me that on Thursday night, she took her father's gun, drove over to her boss' house, knocked on the door, and when her boss answered the door, she fired the gun."

"We never got a call about a shooting," the Sheriff said.

"That's because there wasn't one. The gun wasn't loaded. JoJo's boss took the gun away from her, brought her inside his house, and called her parents. They worked out a deal. If JoJo got professional help, her boss wouldn't press charges."

"Who the hell was she working for?" Berkson asked.

53

"Pastor Paul McCarthy, from Peace Church. He promised to never tell anyone. He knows Dr. McKenzie, who runs a clinic in Kansas City. He helped make the arrangements for JoJo to be admitted. Her parents packed up a few of her things and drove her there the next day. This is the first time, in three years, that she's been home on leave. She's better, but will probably never be one hundred percent. In all likelihood, she'll probably spend the rest of her life there. Her parents figure she'll never be able to function on her own."

"McKenzie. She thinks she was recruited to participate in a project called the McKenzie Experiment," said the Sheriff.

"I'm having trouble wrapping my head around this," said Funtelli. "One day she was normal and the next day she just snapped."

"She thinks she's getting married, you know," the Sheriff said.

"I know. To that Dr. McKenzie. How sad is that?" Funtelli said.

"You put all this behind you three years ago, Simon. Just leave it there and get on with your life. You hear me?"

"I hear you. But, it's a lot easier to say than do."

"You're on leave, Funtelli. Why not pack up your

truck and go fishing. It will give you time to think about things and clear your head. I hear the bass in Mozingo Lake are practically jumping into the boats."

Funtelli sat back in his chair, considering what the Sheriff had said. "I have some vacation days coming. Would you be open to me taking the rest of the week off?"

"If you think that is what you need right now, go for it. Get your head together and just relax. I don't want to see you again until next week."

"Thanks. I appreciate it," Funtelli said.

"Just make sure you bring me back some fish."

Chapter Eight

Bobby Johnson finally felt safe. He was out of the hospital and being cared for in his own home. Charlie Hoppe had taken over a spare bedroom in Bobby's house, so he could see to Bobby's needs, and was on call 24/7.

Bobby's home, the most expensive mobile home money could buy, sat on five acres of land. Except for an area that had been cleared for an Olympic-sized pool and a quarter acre of lawn, the land in back of his home was heavily wooded. John Luke and Sammy were doing twelve-hour shifts, walking the perimeter, and guarding the property. They had asked Bobby to get another guy to help out, so they could cut back to eight hours each. Charlie was working on finding someone.

Dr. Messenly had agreed to make house calls, to check on Bobby's progress. The doctor told Bobby that he would have to be in his cast for a while, but as soon as the leg healed sufficiently, he would be able to hobble around on crutches.

Katie Cuddihey's wake was on Wednesday and her funeral was scheduled for Thursday afternoon. Charlie had ordered flowers, per Bobby's request, to be delivered to the funeral home. Bobby knew Katie's favorite flowers were red carnations, and he had told Charlie to make

56

sure that the arrangement included at least six dozen of them.

Bobby was sleeping a lot. He figured it was the pain medication that made him so tired, but it did the trick and his leg was pain-free most of the time. Plus, when he slept, he didn't think about Katie. He had broken his own rule to never mess with a married woman and it had gotten her killed. It seemed like ages ago that Cal Cuddihey had tried to kill the three of them. Three days, Bobby thought. It's only been three days, and our lives have been changed forever.

He wondered if it would do any good if he tried to talk to Cal. He knew Cal wanted him dead and would probably try again. He figured – no, he knew – that one of them was gonna wind up dead, and he hoped he could nip it in the bud before Cal's hostility went any further. Maybe pay him off. Bobby figured a million would take care of it. He hated to part with the money, but if Cal could see the logic in accepting the money it would be worth it. Cal was going to have a problem paying the bills now, without Katie there to help out. Her income was gone and Cal was going to have to pay a babysitter to watch the kids while he was at work.

Bobby yawned. As he started to settle back under the covers, he glanced over at the bedroom window and noticed someone walking outside. He figured it was either John Luke or Sammy. He wasn't sure who was on duty right now.

"Charlie, are you here?" he called out, at the same time the doorbell rang.

"I'll be right there, Bobby. Someone's at the door."

Bobby could hear the voices but couldn't understand what was being said. He heard the front door shut and waited. Charlie walked into his room, carrying a huge bouquet of flowers.

"That was a delivery service," Charlie said. "They were asked to pick this up at the funeral home and return it to you."

"Are those the flowers we ordered for Katie's funeral?" Bobby asked.

"Looks like it," replied Charlie. "It's got a lot of red carnations in it."

Charlie set the flowers down on a dresser. "Wait, it looks like a card is stuck in here."

"The card I sent?"

"Probably. Let me check." Charlie took the card out of the envelope and looked at it. "Shit."

"What?" Bobby said, loudly. "Read it to me."

Charlie read it to him. "You might want to save these for your own funeral – coming soon." He glanced over at Bobby. "You really should call the police, Bobby. This is getting out of hand."

"We've just got to give him some time to settle down. I betrayed him. I messed around with my best friend's wife. Of course, he wants to get even."

"He wants to kill you. That's what he wants, Bobby. Please, reconsider."

"I'll think about it. I'm tired and I need a shot. Will you ask my nurse to get the hell out of my pool and get her ass in here? Who's working right now, anyway? It's not Nancy. What's her name again?"

"Betty Lou."

"That's right. Will you get her for me?"

Charlie motioned towards the floral arrangement. "What do you want me to do with this?"

"Throw the damn thing out."

As Charlie reached for them, Bobby held up his hand. "Wait. They kinda brighten up the room, don't they? Leave 'em. Just take that wrapping off so they can spread out."

"You want to leave them here on the dresser?" Charlie asked as he removed the paper.

"The dresser is fine. Now go get that nurse in here, will you?"

"I'm on it. Be right back," Charlie replied.

Sheriff Berkson was surprised to see Dr. Wasserstein walk into the station. "Hey, Doc. What can I do for you?"

"Hey, Cowboy. I need to talk to you about Bobby Johnson."

"I heard he went home from the hospital already. That was fast."

"Not my choice. He wanted to go home, and he made his own arrangements. He hired some paramedics to take him home from the hospital. Dr. Messenly is quite concerned about his leaving like that, but he's getting round-the-clock care, so he'll probably be okay."

"What's the problem, then?"

"Something is going on with him. Did you know that he made arrangements to have someone sit guard outside his room at the hospital? He's afraid of someone, and I think it might be Cal Cuddihey."

"What makes you think that?" Sheriff Berkson inquired.

"Cuddihey got close to Bobby's room in the hospital and Sammy Severson, who was guarding Bobby, had a little tussle with him. One of the nurses said Cuddihey made a threatening gesture at Bobby."

"Like what?"

Dr. Wasserstein made a fist, stuck out his index finger, and pretended to shot a gun. "Like that. Something's going on, Sheriff. I'm beginning to think that boat hitting the dock may not have been an accident."

"You think Cal Cuddihey ran that boat into the dock on purpose? That's a little crazy, don't you think?"

"There's a rumor going around that Bobby might have been a little too friendly with Katie. Perhaps Charlie intended to kill everybody on that boat, including himself."

"Come on, Doc. Anyway, if Charlie had tried to kill him, why wouldn't Bobby say something?" Berkson asked.

"Guilt, perhaps, if the rumor is true. Maybe he's hiding something. Who knows? I just thought you should know. Perhaps, you can talk to him."

"You mean Bobby?" asked the Sheriff.

"Ya, Bobby."

"Did Cal's test results come back yet?" Berkson inquired, changing the subject.

"They were clean. No sign of any epilepsy or any reason for him to have a seizure. He wasn't drunk. We don't know what happened?"

"Motor freeze up?" the Sheriff contemplated.

"I was told the insurance company is checking all that out. But, right now, we just don't know."

"I've known you for a long time, Doc. If you think something is going on, I believe you. I'll look into it. Bobby Johnson and Cal Cuddihey have been friends for years, though. Maybe Cal was just goofing around when he made that gesture," said the Sheriff.

"So, why did Bobby want a guard outside his room?"

"Good question," replied the Sheriff. "I'll definitely have a talk with Bobby."

"Thanks," said Dr. Wasserstein.

"You wanna go have some lunch?" Sheriff Berkson asked.

"Sorry, I've got to get to the hospital. I'll take a rain check on that, though."

"You got it. I'll let you know what I find out."

As Sheriff Berkson watched the doctor leave his office, he wondered what the hell was going on now. The last thing he needed was another murder in Hollister. He figured the sooner he talked to Bobby, the better.

Chapter Nine

Nurse Betty Lou Harrison was standing at the foot of Bobby's bed. Before she walked into his room, he had every intention of chewing her out. He wasn't prepared, however, for her to be practically naked. So, right now, chewing her out was the last thing he was thinking about.

Betty Lou was drop-dead gorgeous. Earlier in the day, Bobby hadn't paid much attention to her when she gave him a shot. But, right now, seeing her standing in front of him in a bikini that barely covered her private parts, he was paying a lot of attention. In fact, he was standing at attention. He reached down, grabbed his blanket, and threw it over himself, hoping she had not seen his reaction.

"You need something, Bobby?" she practically purred. "What can little ol' Betty Lou do for you?"

Bobby looked her up and down, grinning. "That bikini doesn't leave a whole lot to the imagination, does it?"

Betty Lou softly laughed. "Do you like it?"

"I do. You know what? You just perked up my day."

"I did? I'm so glad I did that. And, Bobby, I'm pretty sure I perked up more than just your day.

63

Bobby laughed. "You sure did. You know what, Betty Lou? I'd love to continue this conversation, but I'm hurting pretty bad. I think I'm way past due for a shot."

Betty Lou glanced at her watch. "Why, you sure are. I'm sorry. I was enjoying your pool so much, I totally lost track of time. Can you roll over on your side? This one's going in your left cheek."

"I think I can manage that," Bobby said.

"I'll be right back, Sweetie. Got to go get the meds."

Bobby watched her walk out of the room. He grinned, thinking about Betty Lou's comment. He was pretty sure he was going to get a blow job before the day was over,

Charlie was in the living room watching TV. He smiled when Betty Lou came out of Bobby's bedroom and walked into the kitchen. He enjoyed the little show she was putting on as much as the next guy, but it was gonna stop right now. He got up and followed her. She glanced over at him and continued to get the morphine shot ready to give to Bobby.

"You will get dressed before you go back into Bobby's room."

"Excuse me?" Betty Lou said.

"You are being paid for your services. That does

64

not include enjoying Bobby's pool. Nor, does it mean that you're gonna do your job in a bathing suit. If you can even call it that. You are to remain in the house while on duty, properly dressed. Your job is to make sure that Bobby is comfortable and that's your only job. Got it?"

"I think I've been a nurse long enough to know what my patients need."

"How much are you being paid an hour?" Charlie asked her.

"I was told I'm getting $60.00 an hour," she replied.

"And, who hired you?"

"Bobby did."

"No, Betty Lou. He did not. I did. I hired you and I can fire you. Now, you can start acting professionally and earn your $480.00 a day for the next six or eight weeks, or you can get your sorry ass out of here right now. Understand?"

"Well, I'll just see what Bobby has to say about that."

"No, you won't. You're fired."

Betty Lou threw the syringe down on the table. "Just how do you think Bobby's gonna get his shot now?"

Charlie smiled. "That's not your problem, anymore. Do you want me to walk you to your car or can you manage?"

Betty Lou gave him a dirty look. "I'm going. Just as soon as I change clothes and say goodbye to Bobby."

Charlie walked over and took her by the arm. "It looks like you might need some help. Let's go or do you want me to get Sammy in here to carry you to your car?"

Betty Lou shook his hand loose. "I'm going. You're a real bastard, Charlie. You know that?"

"I've been told that a few times."

Betty Lou walked to the spare bedroom and grabbed her clothes and purse off the bed. She slipped on a pair of sandals and headed towards the front door. As she opened it, she found herself face to face with Sheriff Berkson. Startled, she took a step backwards.

"Excuse me, ma'am. I didn't mean to scare you."

"Fuck you," she said to the Sheriff and pushed past him.

"Sorry about that, Sheriff," said Charlie, laughing. "It's hard to get good help these days."

"Especially help that looks like that," said the Sheriff.

"Are you here to see Bobby?"

"I'd like to talk to him, if he's awake."

66

"He's awake. But, talk fast. I'm about to give him a shot. Once he gets that pain medication, he's out for a few hours."

"Okay to go in his room?"

'Go ahead. Tell him I'll be right there.

Bobby smiled and turned his head towards the door, expecting to see Betty Lou. His smile quickly disappeared when he saw Sheriff Berkson.

"Where's Betty Lou?" Bobby asked. "She's supposed to give me my shot."

"You'll have to ask Charlie about that," replied the Sheriff. "You got a minute? I'd like to talk to you."

"About what?" Bobby asked.

"I'd like to know what's going on, Bobby. I've heard that you had security guarding you while you were in the hospital. What was that all about?"

"Just taking a few precautions, that's all. No big deal."

"Well, then, perhaps you can tell me why Sammy Severson is walking around outside your house, carrying a shotgun? What are you afraid of?"

"Like I said, Sheriff. Just being careful."

"Did Cal Cuddihey threaten you?"

"Excuse me a minute, Sheriff." He turned towards

the door and yelled for Charlie.

Charlie stuck his head in and asked, "Whataya need?"

"My friggin' shot. Where the hell is Betty Lou with my pain medication?

"I'm giving you the shot just as soon as the Sheriff is done talking to you."

"I believe we're done." Bobby looked at the Sheriff. "Is there anything else you need?" he asked.

"You gonna answer my question, Bobby?"

"Nobody threatened me. I'm fine. Now, if you don't mind, I'd like you to leave. I'm in pain here and I need my medication."

Sheriff Berkson gave Bobby a stern look. "I know you're keeping something from me. When it gets too much for you to handle, give me a call. And, Bobby. . . "

"What?"

"Don't wait too long. Because, by then, it might be too late."

Bobby laughed nervously. "Nothing to worry about. Like I said, Sheriff, everything is just fine."

As Sheriff Berkson turned to leave the room, he noticed the floral arrangement on Bobby's dresser. "Someone must really like you. Those are beautiful flowers."

"They are, aren't they?" Bobby softly agreed.

"I'll see myself out," said the Sheriff. "Give me a call if you need anything."

"Thanks," Bobby replied and watched Berkson leave his room.

"Where the hell is Betty Lou?" he asked Charlie, raising his voice.

"She left. She said she had an emergency. I guess it was a family thing."

"Are you shitting me?"

"Roll over on your side," said Charlie.

"Why?"

"I'm giving you your shot. I believe it's the left cheek this time."

Bobby rolled onto his right side. "You sure you know what you're doing?" he asked.

"Of course, I know what I'm doing. What? You forgot I was a medic when I was in the Army?"

"What really happened to Betty Lou?"

"I fired her. She has a smart mouth and she wasn't very good at her job."

"The only job I was hoping she'd be good at was a blow job. You should have checked with me before you fired her.

Charlie laughed and gave Bobby his shot. "I'll let

you make the decisions when you're off the morphine. Right now, roll over and get some rest."

"Thanks, Charlie."

Charlie sat down in a big overstuffed chair, close to Bobby's bed, and watched him until he fell asleep.

Chapter Ten

The flowers, in the floral arrangement on top of the dresser, slowly moved. A light brownish-gray head with a black stripe looked over the edge of the vase. It slithered out of its encasement, landing on top of the dresser. It remained there, motionless for a few seconds, and then dropped to the floor. It sounded its rattle and flicked its tongue in and out, sensing danger.

A few seconds later, two more small snakes emerged from the floral arrangement and joined the snake on the floor. Silently, they glided across the rug, making their way towards Charlie. They sounded their rattles, which mimicked a faint buzz like the sound of a grasshopper.

Charlie stirred as the buzzing sound disturbed his slumber, decided it was nothing, settled comfortably back into the chair, and fell back to sleep. A few minutes later, he felt a sharp sting on his right leg. He reached down and was immediately struck in the back of his hand. Before he could pull his hand out of the way, he was bitten once more. He cried out but Bobby, who was in a deep morphine-induced sleep, did not hear him. Within seconds, Charlie was unconscious.

Bobby's nightmare woke him. He was wet with

sweat and his heart was pounding. The room was dark. He wondered how long he had been sleeping. He clapped twice and a light, next to his bed, came on.

Bobby was dying of thirst. He glanced over at a water glass sitting on the nightstand. The glass was empty. Then, he noticed Charlie sleeping in a chair across the room. He was just about to wake him when he heard a faint buzz. Bobby hesitated and listened for a couple of seconds, wondering where the sound was coming from. Deciding the noise was just some night critter rubbing its legs together, he turned his attention back to Charlie.

"Charlie," he called out. "Wake up."

Charlie didn't respond. "Charlie," he yelled. "Wake your sorry ass up. I need some water."

Again, there was no response from Charlie. Just as he was about to yell the third time, Wally Weatherwax, his night nurse came into the room.

"You're finally awake," Wally said. "That was one hell of a nap."

"What time is it?" Bobby asked.

"It's three o'clock."

"In the morning?"

Wally laughed. "Like I said, you had one hell of a long nap. Charlie, too. He's still sleeping."

72

Bobby looked over at Charlie, suddenly sensing that something wasn't right. "I think something's wrong with him. Wake him up," Bobby yelled.

As Wally started towards Charlie, he yelled, "Snake! I saw a snake," and ran out of the room.

"Where?" Bobby yelled. "Where is it?"

"There." Wally stuck his head around the corner of the doorway and pointed. "Next to Charlie's foot. Do you see it?"

Bobby slowly opened up the drawer in his nightstand, pulled out a gun, and fired.

"You killed it," yelled Wally. "Oh, my god, I was so scared."

"I think Charlie's been bit."

Wally went over to Charlie and checked his pulse. "He's alive, but his pulse is really slow. I'm calling 911. He needs help."

"Tell them he was bit by a Western Pygmy Rattler. It probably bit him more than once, or he wouldn't be out like that. Wait. It'll be faster if you drive him to the hospital. I'll call and tell them you're bringing him in."

"You're right," said Wally. "I'll get John Luke to help me put him in the car." He ran out of the room, opened the front door, and screamed for John Luke.

John Luke ran into the house, holding his

73

shotgun. "You okay, Bobby? What's the matter?"

"It's Charlie. He's been bit by a snake and needs help. You and Wally put him in your truck and get him to the hospital," Bobby said.

"That snake bite won't kill him," John Luke said.

"He's kinda in bad shape," Bobby said. "I think it just might."

Bobby watched as John Luke and Wally carried Charlie out of the room. "Wally, I want you to stay here with me. Got it?"

"Got it," Wally said. "I'll be back as soon as we get Charlie in the truck."

"Bring me a drink of water, will you?" Bobby yelled as he heard the front door shut. "And, put some ice in it."

"Be right there," Wally yelled back.

Bobby picked up the TV remote and turned on the TV. He flipped from channel to channel, trying to find something besides an infomercial. Suddenly, he heard the sound of breaking glass followed by Wally screaming, "Snakes!"

Wally came tearing through Bobby's bedroom door and jumped up on his bed. "Shoot them," Wally yelled.

"There's another snake in the house?" Bobby

asked.

"Two more! I saw two more!"

"Did you get bit?"

"No. Oh, my god. I'm shaking. I hate snakes more than anything," Wally said and started to cry.

"Call the police and tell them to get out here."

"My phone's in the living room. I'm not getting off the bed."

"Use mine. It's on the nightstand," Bobby said. "I don't get it. Where the hell did the snakes come from?"

"OMG!" Wally yelled.

"Now what?"

"The flowers are . . ." Wally looked at Bobby. "Your house is haunted, isn't it? Did someone put a spell on you?" He let out a piercing scream as he stared at the floral arrangement. "Look at those flowers. They're moving. See that?" he yelled, as he pointed his finger at the dresser.

Bobby reached over to his nightstand and grabbed his cell phone. He tossed it at Wally and said, "Call 911. Tell them to get here right now."

Then he picked up his gun and shot the hell out of the floral arrangement.

Chapter Eleven

John Luke called Sammy from the hospital, told him what had happened to Charlie, and asked him to get out to Bobby's ASAP. Sammy, still not quite wide awake or completely sure what was going on, pulled up in front of Bobby's, grabbed his shotgun, and ran to the house. He opened the front door and found himself face to face with a rattlesnake.

"Whoa," he cried out and stepped back, tripped over his own feet, fell backwards, and tumbled down the steps. He sat on the ground for a few seconds to clear his head and then got up. The small snake was crossing over the threshold and slithering down the steps. Sammy looked around for his shotgun and saw it lying on the porch. He took a few steps back, watched the snake crawl down the steps and disappear into the grass.

"Hate those damn things," he said and walked back up the steps. As he reached down to pick up his shotgun, he saw another snake crawling towards him. Bringing the butt of the gun down hard, he smashed its head.

"Who's out there?" Bobby yelled from his bedroom.

"What the hell is going on here, Bobby?" Sammy said as he walked into Bobby's bedroom. He stopped

76

when he saw Wally, curled up at the end of Bobby's bed, sniffling. He looked questioningly at Bobby.

"It's been a rough night," said Bobby, smiling.

"No shit," said Sammy, as he surveyed the damage in the bedroom. "What'd that dresser ever do to you?"

"Did you see any snakes when you came in?" Bobby replied, ignoring the sarcasm.

"A couple. Killed one. The other one got away. Want me to put out an APB?"

"Funny. That may be all of them. Hey, Wally, how about getting off my bed? I think all snakes are gone."

"No way," replied Wally.

"Sammy, would you look around and check to see if any more snakes are roaming around?"

"Looks like the cops are here," said Sammy, seeing red and blue lights flashing through the window. "Did you call them?"

"I figured we might need them. Tell them everything's under control. The last thing I need right now is to have to try to explain how a bunch of snakes got in the house."

"How did they get in?" Sammy asked.

"Best I can figure out is that they were in that floral arrangement."

"How'd they get in there?" Wally asked.

77

"Never you mind. It's not important. How about getting me that nice cold glass of water now? And, clean up that broken glass in the kitchen."

"Is it safe to get off the bed?" Wally asked Sammy.

"Should be. That's the police knocking. I'll be right back."

Wally waited until Sammy answered the front door before he jumped off the bed and ran out of the room. "I'm out of here. I'll get my stuff in a few days," he shouted at Bobby, as he made a mad dash for the front door.

"Where are you going?" Bobby yelled at him.

"I quit. I sure as hell ain't working in no haunted house." He brushed past Sammy and Officer Bell and ran for his car.

"There're snakes out there," Sammy yelled at Wally. "Better watch where you're running." He laughed, as Wally did the high step all the way to his car.

Officer Zeke Bell watched Wally get into his car and burn rubber as he tore out of the driveway. "What's the problem here, Sammy? And, who was that?"

"Sorry, Zeke. That was Wally Weatherwax. Bobby hired him as his night shift nurse and it turned out he's terrified of snakes. One found its way into the house and he freaked out and called you. We got the snake and everything's okay. Again, we're sorry to have bothered you, but everything's fine here."

"Maybe I should go talk to Bobby," Officer Bell said.

"I don't think it's necessary to bother him. He's probably sleeping."

"You sure you don't need me to check around and make sure everything's all right?"

"Positive. We're all good."

"All right, then. Call me if you need anything."

"Will do, Zeke. Thanks again," said Sammy. He watched the cop drive off, then, walked back into the house, closing and locking the door behind him.

"Is he gone?" Bobby asked.

"Yep. You okay?"

"Been better. How's Charlie? Have you heard from John Luke?"

"Not yet. What the hell happened in here, Bobby? It looks like a war zone."

"It's not easy shooting snakes when you're lying in bed. Besides the broken glass here from the mirror, there's glass all over the kitchen floor. Would you mind getting a wastebasket and cleaning up the mess?"

Looking confused, Sammy didn't say anything for a few seconds. He looked at Bobby, and asked, "How many snakes altogether, did you say?"

"Five, I think. I'm not exactly sure how many were in that arrangement, but I think there were five altogether."

"Uh, huh. So, you telling me that five snakes just happened to be in that arrangement?"

"Looks like it," said Bobby.

"And, just how do you think they got in there, Bobby?"

"I have an idea."

"You wanna tell me?"

"You gonna keep it quiet? Not blab it all over town?" Bobby asked him.

"I can keep my mouth shut," Sammy told him.

"Cal."

"Cal Cuddihey?"

"Yep."

"Why would he send you flowers with snakes in the vase? That don't make no sense to me."

"He's pissed off at me, Sammy. That's the floral arrangement I had delivered for Katie's wake at the funeral home. He sent it back to me. I figure he put the snakes in it."

"He must really be pissed off to do that. That's why you had us guarding you at the hospital, isn't it?

You said to keep him away from you, but I didn't think he was actually gonna try to kill you."

"You figure you can get this mess cleaned up?"

"I'm on it. Anything else?"

"Call John Luke and see how Charlie is doing?"

Chapter Twelve

"Morning, Sheriff," Deputy Casey George said, as he walked into the police station. "What's on the menu this morning?"

"Nothing special. It looks pretty routine right now."

"Quiet night?"

"Pretty much. Zeke was called out to Bobby Johnson's place. False alarm, though. Seems a snake got in the house and Bobby's nurse panicked. Zeke said the nurse – a male nurse, by the way - went running out of the house yelling that he quit and something about the house being haunted."

"Don't know many people who do like snakes. You just have to learn to stay clear of them and they'll mostly leave you alone," said Casey. "Anything else happen?"

"Not much. A few traffic violations. We got Pete Drollberg in the cage for drunk and disorderly."

"On a Tuesday night? That's unusual for him. He mostly pulls that crap on a Saturday night."

"It seems him and the missus got into a battle about some dumb thing. He stormed out of the house, went to a bar, and had a few too many," the Sheriff said.

"Usually is some dumb thing. You and Sarah never fight, do you?"

"Did a couple of times when we were first married. I found out I wasn't real good at it. I never won. So, I learned to keep my mouth shut and a smile on my face."

"I wish Betsy would learn to cook like Sarah. Especially, her meatloaf. Do you think Sarah would give her the recipe?"

"I could ask her."

"Thanks, Sheriff."

Sheriff Berkson reached over and picked up the phone. "Hollister Police Department."

He frowned as listened to the voice on the other end. "Are you sure there were three?" he inquired. He was quiet for a few more minutes and, then, asked, "What time was he brought in?"

Deputy George listened to the one-sided conversation and deduced that the Sheriff was talking to someone at the hospital. He started to say something to Berkson, but the Sheriff motioned for him to be quiet.

"Is he still there?" Berkson asked. He listened for a few more seconds, said, "Thanks for letting me know," and hung up the phone.

"What?" asked Casey.

"Charlie Hoppe was brought into emergency around four o'clock this morning. He had three snake bites and was in pretty bad shape."

83

"Three? It's unusual for a snake to bite you three times," said Casey.

"Or, maybe there was more than one snake," replied the Sheriff.

"What time was Zeke called out to Bobby's last night?"

"I believe the report said around three-thirty." Sheriff Berkson gave Casey a questioning look. "I wonder what the hell was going on in that house last night. What made that nurse go running out of there so terrified that he quit his job? It had to be more than just one little snake in the house. I tell you, Casey, there's a lot more going on with Bobby Johnson than he's letting on."

"You gonna go talk to Charlie?" Casey asked him.

"He already left the hospital. The emergency doctor got him stable and wanted to admit him, but he refused. He left about thirty minutes ago."

"You think this has something to do with Cal Cuddihey, don't you?"

"I got a feeling, that's all. Doc Wasserstein thinks something is going on and I'm beginning to think he might just be onto something."

"You gonna drive out to Bobby's?"

"Later on. Maybe now, after whatever the hell was

going on there last night, he'll be ready to tell me the truth."

"Can I go with you?" Casey asked.

"I guess. Why?"

"I don't know. I guess I'm just curious to see what he has to say. Besides, it looks like it's gonna be a boring day."

"I like it like that. Boring is good, Casey," said the Sheriff.

Charlie was standing alongside Bobby's bed, looking down at the floor. "You sure you got all those fuckers?" Charlie asked.

"No, I'm not. I want you to call Donny Ray and ask him to bring Thor over. If there's a snake left in this house, that dog will sniff it out."

"Good idea. I'll call him right now."

"If he can't bring him, see if it'll be okay if John Luke can go pick him up," said Bobby.

"Where's Sammy?" asked Charlie.

"I sent him home to get some sleep. We definitely need to get one more guy to help stand guard. You know anyone who's looking to make a few bucks?" asked Bobby.

"I'll check around. I heard Phil Wilson is out of

work. Maybe he'll be interested, plus he's a great shot."

"Hopefully, it won't come to that. I called Nancy and told her to take the second shift today. I'm overdue for a pain shot. You up to giving me one?"

"Absolutely. Give me a minute. I'll be right back."

"Also, Charlie, we need a couple of new nurses."

"A couple?"

"Wally had a hissy fit about the snakes and quit. Can't say I blame him. It was complete chaos here last night."

"I'm on it, right after I give you a shot."

"Look out for snakes," Bobby said, as Charlie started to leave the room.

"Ha-ha. Aren't you funny?" Charlie said, laughing.

Donny Ray and Thor were just pulling away when Sheriff Berkson and Deputy George arrived at Bobby's house. John Luke greeted them as they got out of the squad car and told them to go on in.

Charlie Hoppe looked up as the door opened, told someone he was talking to on his phone that he'd call them back, and ended the call.

"Afternoon, Sheriff. Deputy. Whataya doing here?" Charlie asked.

"Just checking to see how Bobby's doing today. I

heard Officer Bell got called out here last night and I'm following up to be sure everything's okay."

"We had a little snake problem, but it's been taken care of," Charlie said.

"I heard you got bit a few times and wound up in emergency. How are you doing?"

"News sure travels fast."

"Small town, Charlie."

"I'm fine. Those Pygmy Rattlers might be small but they sure as hell pack a powerful punch."

"Unusual for one of them to strike three times," said the Sheriff.

"There was more than one," said Charlie.

"How many do you figure?" asked the Sheriff.

"A couple, I guess."

"How'd they get in the house?" the Sheriff inquired.

"No idea."

"Heard you lost one of Bobby's nurses, too."

"The snakes scared him off. No problem, there. I've already hired a replacement."

"Okay if I go look in on Bobby?"

"He's asleep. Those shots knock him out for a few hours."

"He still in a lot of pain?" the Sheriff asked.

"It's a little better, but he's still hurting. Dr. Messenly will be out later. Hopefully, he'll take him off those shots. A couple of pain pills will do the same thing."

"I saw John Luke outside. What's he carrying a shotgun for?"

Charlie looked away for a few seconds, thinking about his answer. "We heard a bear's been roaming around and getting into people's garbage," he finally said.

"I haven't heard about that," replied the Sheriff.

"Just a rumor goin' around."

"Well, guess we'll be going. Call if you need anything." The Sheriff started towards the door, with Casey following him. Suddenly, the Sheriff turned and walked towards Bobby's bedroom.

"I think Bobby's awake. I'll say hello to him before we leave," he said to Charlie.

"I don't think you should disturb him," Charlie said.

"I'll just be a minute."

Sheriff Berkson walked into Bobby's bedroom. Bobby was asleep and snoring. He glanced around the room and noticed that the floral arrangement was no longer on the dresser. He saw what he was sure were

88

bullet holes in the top of the dresser and that the mirror was shattered. He checked the walls and ceiling but didn't see any damage. As he turned to leave the room, he glanced down at the floor and noticed some red spots on the carpet. He knelt down and gave it a closer look. He was pretty sure it was blood.

He left the room and joined his deputy and Charlie, who were talking in the living room.

"Where'd the blood on the rug in there come from?" he asked Charlie.

"That's snake blood. Bobby killed it after it bit me."

"Do you mind if we take a sample and test it?" the Sheriff asked him.

"Hell, no. Be my guest."

"Casey, go get the kit from the car and take a sample of that blood on the carpet in there."

"Sure thing, Sheriff," Casey replied.

"What happened to the floral arrangement that was on the dresser? And, don't tell me the flowers died already."

"It got knocked off the dresser and broke, so Sammy threw it out."

"Bullshit, Charlie. There's no bear roaming around and that arrangement didn't just fall off the dresser.

89

How about you tell me what the hell went on here last night."

"I got bit by a snake and John Luke took me to emergency. I have no idea what happened here after that. I wasn't here," he replied.

"The devil you don't know. Something's going on with Bobby and I want to know what it is."

"You'll have to ask Bobby," Charlie replied, looking at the floor.

"Is Cal Cuddihey after him?" the Sheriff asked.

Charlie's head jerked up in surprise. "Why'd you ask that?"

"There's a rumor going 'round," said the Sheriff, mimicking Charlie. "So, is he?"

"I guess you'll have to ask Bobby about that, too. Is there anything else you need before you leave?" Charlie asked the Sheriff.

"I'd like some answers, Charlie. Somebody better tell me what's going on before it's too late."

"Like I said, Sheriff, you'll have to talk to Bobby."

Sheriff Berkson gave him a disgusted look. "If anything happens, it's on you, Charlie."

"Nothing's gonna happen, Sheriff. There's nothing going on."

"Are you done in there?" the Sheriff yelled at

Casey.

"Coming," Casey answered.

Sheriff Berkson and Casey headed for the door. The Sheriff turned and looked at Charlie. "You know what I'd really like to know, Charlie?"

"What's that, Sheriff?"

"I'd like to know why, every time there's trouble here in Hollister, Bobby Johnson is right in the middle of it all."

Charlie smiled. "Guess he just has a bad habit of being in the wrong place at the wrong time. See ya, Sheriff."

Floating Face Down - - - - - - - Susan L. Pare'

<u>Chapter Thirteen</u>

"You've got some nerve, calling me."

"We need to talk," Bobby said.

"I'm burying my wife in a few hours, and you want to talk? Go to hell, Bobby."

"You wouldn't be burying her if you hadn't killed her."

"Like I said, Bobby. You go to hell."

"Cal, for god's sake, this has got to end. What do you want? What can I do that will make you stop this nonsense?"

"What do I want? You can't give me what I want. I want my life back. I want things like they were before you started banging my wife."

"I'm sorry. That was a mistake, Cal. I'm so very sorry. But, killing me isn't going to make things better. You've got kids, for crying out loud. Think about what you're doing."

"Oh, I'm thinking about it all right. All I do is think about how I can kill you. They say the third time is the charm, Bobby. I plan to find out real soon."

"I'm gonna give you an option, Cal. You stop this crap, step back, and get on with your life. I'll set up college funds for Calli and Patrick, so you don't have to worry about their education. Or – and, I mean this – I'll tell the police what happened last Sunday. You killed your wife and you almost killed me. I seriously don't want to see you in jail and your kids losing both their parents, but this shit has got to end. It's time for you to back off."

"You seriously think you can buy me off or threaten me? You're an asshole, Bobby. Do you think I care what happens to me? I wish I'd died in that crash, too. I wish we all had. Go tell the police what happened. I don't care. It's your word against mine now."

"Is there anything I can do to make this right, Cal?" Bobby asked.

Cal didn't say anything for a few seconds. "You know what, Bobby? There is."

"Anything. Just tell me."

"You can stick a gun in your mouth and blow your fucking brains out. That's what you can do. I gotta go. It's time to bury that cheating bitch."

Bobby lay back in his bed and closed his eyes. Well, at least I tried, he thought. It looks like it's gonna be Cal or me, 'cause if this crap continues one of us is gonna wind up dead, for sure.

He recalled how Katie had looked in that orange bikini. It had been a fun day, drinking beer with Cal, watching the kids splashing around in the pool, and cooking out. Katie had spent the entire afternoon in that bikini. It was obvious that every move she made was meant to tease him and it had worked. By the time the day was over, all Bobby could think of was making love to her.

He called her four days later and asked if she'd like to bring the kids over for a swim, seeing how they had enjoyed the pool so much a couple of days ago. She had told him that her kids were spending a few days with their grandparents and wouldn't be home until Sunday. When he had jokingly asked if she might like to put on that sexy bikini and join him in the pool, she had said yes.

Bobby smiled as he thought about that afternoon. She never made it into that bikini and they never made it into the pool. She was a wild one, he thought. From the minute she stepped into his house until she left three hours later, she never quit touching him. Bobby was left undeniably satiated, totally exhausted, and wanting more. He couldn't get her out of his head, and just the thought of her made him hard.

She called her parents and asked if they would keep the kids for a little longer. When they said yes, she called Bobby and told him that he better rest up. He was in for a rough week.

She was there five times that week. He couldn't wait for her to arrive and couldn't stand it when she walked out of the door to go home.

He begged her to leave Cal and move in with him. She had laughed, when he said that, and told him to enjoy today and not worry about tomorrow.

On the fifth day, as she was leaving, she turned to him and told him that it was over. I enjoyed it, Bobby, she had said. It was a lot of fun. I just don't want to take any more chances that Cal might find out about us.

Bobby had begged her to change her mind. He would marry her and take care of her kids, anything she wanted, if she would only stay with him. She kissed him on his cheek, told him she thought he was sweet, and left.

He didn't find out that Cal knew about their affair until last Sunday. Cal had called Bobby and asked if he had any plans for the day. Calli and Patrick were spending the day with Katie's sister. The weather forecast said it was going to be hot and sunny. He wondered if Bobby would like to take him and Katie out on his boat. Katie will pack a lunch, he told Bobby, and I'll bring the booze. Bobby jumped at the chance to spend the day with his friend and his wife.

Bobby started out driving the boat, but after a few drinks, he asked Cal to take over the wheel. Cal wasn't a big drinker and he had readily agreed, commenting about Bobby not being able to hold his liquor. Bobby had laughed at that and said that he sure could and he usually held her by her ears. He remembered that Cal hadn't laughed at his joke.

Bobby continued drinking. It was hot, he hadn't eaten breakfast, and it didn't take long before he was half out of it. Katie said she thought it might be a good idea if they stopped somewhere and had something to eat.

Suddenly, in the middle of the lake, Cal shut off the engine, turned, and glared at Bobby and Katie.

"What's the matter?" Bobby had asked. "You look like you just swallowed sour milk."

"You're an ass, Bobby."

Bobby had laughed and taken another swallow of his drink. Then, he wiped the grin from his face, realizing Cal was serious.

"What's your problem?" Bobby had asked Cal.

"You. And, that bitch sitting back there. You two are my problem."

"Don't you call me a bitch," Katie had yelled at Cal.

"My best friend and my wife fucking. Did you really think you'd get away with it?"

"I don't know what you're talking about," Bobby had responded.

"Don't play dumb with me, Bobby. Katie's car was seen parked on the side of your house. Not just once, either, but several times. You two are so stupid. You didn't even have enough sense to try to hide it. You wanna tell me what she was doing there if you weren't fucking? I know she wasn't there to clean your house, Bobby. She hates to clean. She hardly cleans our house. Or, maybe she was cleaning your pipes. Am I right, Bobby? Is that what she was doing?

"You don't know what you're talking about, Cal,"

"Look me in the eye, Bobby, and tell me you didn't screw my wife."

Bobby had looked away and didn't answer him.

"How about you, Katie? Did you screw my best friend? How many others have there been? I married a whore, Bobby. Did you know that?"

"Cal, please stop this. You've got this all wrong," Bobby had told him.

Cal looked at him, tears rolling down his cheeks. "You're a no-good son of a bitch, Bobby. You were my best friend. How could you do this to me?"

98

"Cal, I'm sorry," Bobby had said. "It just happened. I'm so sorry."

Cal had turned away from them, started the boat, and headed towards the shore. Suddenly, he kicked it into full throttle, throwing Bobby and Katie backward. Bobby yelled at Cal to slow down and heard Katie screaming. At the speed they were going, it didn't take long before they crashed into the dock in front of Belle's Waterfront Café.

An involuntary shiver went through Bobby's body as he remembered being thrown from the boat. Funny, he thought. I didn't remember that until just now.

I knew it was wrong, Bobby thought. Cal has every right to want to kill me. I'm sorry that Katie's dead. I'm sorry that I betrayed Cal. But, I'm not just gonna lie in this bed and let Cal kill me. It's time to back off the pain medication, he decided. Fuck Cal's kids. Their daddy needs to go.

Chapter Fourteen

"Hey, look who's back," Deputy George said, as Officer Funtelli walked into the Police Department.

"Hi, Casey. Miss me?"

"Hell, no. Whatcha got in that cooler?"

"Lots of bass. I caught enough so everyone can have a few."

"So, fishing was good up there at Mozingo Lake, was it?"

"Casey, so help me god, the Sheriff was right about the fish practically jumping into the boats. I caught my limit every day."

"I'm glad you had a good time."

"Sheriff here?" Funtelli asked.

"Naw. He's out on a call. He should be back soon."

"Anything exciting happen while I was gone?"

"Not really. The most exciting thing was a call out to Bobby Johnson's house. Seems they had a snake problem, but it was mostly taken care of before Zeke got there."

"How's Bobby doing?"

"Last I heard, he's okay. Katie Cuddihey's funeral was yesterday. Huge turnout. I feel sorry for those two little kids, being left with no mother. Life really sucks sometimes."

"Tell me about it."

"When you coming back to work?" Casey asked him.

"Monday. I still have a few vacation days left. I'm gonna go home, get cleaned up, and head up to Kansas City."

"You just came from that direction. What's going on in Kansas City?"

"JoJo."

Casey looked at Funtelli questioningly and shook his head. "You don't think that's a good idea, do you?"

"I need to talk to her. I only saw her for a few seconds in the bar. I never had a chance to really talk to her."

Funtelli handed Casey the cooler. "Put these in the freezer, will you? You can tell the guys to take what they want."

"She's crazy. You know that, don't you?"

"I need to do this, Casey. I need closure."

"It's been a long time, Simon. You should have had closure by now."

"We thought she was dead. I need to talk to her. I have questions that need to be answered. I need to know what happened. We were in love. I was going to ask her to marry me. What put her over the edge? I'm gonna drive up there and get some answers."

"You're setting yourself up for a big letdown. You might want to rethink this."

"I'll see you on Monday. Tell the Sheriff I said 'hey'."

"Good luck, Simon," Casey said. "I think you're on a fool's journey, but good luck, anyway."

"Thanks. See ya."

Casey watched as Funtelli walked out of the building. "Damn fool," he said. He picked up the cooler and took it into the back room. He opened the refrigerator door, took the frozen fish out of the container, and put them into the freezer compartment.

Dr. Messenly was sitting on a chair next to Bobby's bed. "I want you to understand that if I stop the shots, you're going to experience more pain than you are now. Are you sure about this, Bobby?"

"I'm sure. I don't like sleeping half the day away. I'd rather have a little more pain and be awake. Besides, there are pills I can take, aren't there?"

"Of course. But I'll need to limit the amount you can take. It's easy to get hooked on them. I want you to promise me that you won't exceed the prescribed amount."

"No problem. Just write me a prescription and I'll have Charlie get it filled. How much longer do I have to keep this cast on?"

"It hasn't even been a week, Bobby."

"It's driving me nuts. My leg itches all the time. I want it off."

"How about I make you a removable cast? You can remove it while you're in bed, as long as you don't move around a lot. The rest of the time, it's on. You understand?"

"I understand. Let's do tha . . ." Bobby looked at him. "What do you mean, the rest of the time?"

"I'm going to start you on some physical therapy and crutches next week. We'll get the cast done first."

"So, I'll be mobile next week," Bobby said. He gave the doctor a big grin.

"Don't get too excited, Bobby. You're only going to be allowed a few steps at a time. You'll be able to hobble to the bathroom, but that's about it. At least for a while. You won't be able to put any weight on that leg yet. It's gonna take time and you're gonna have to be patient."

"Thanks, Doc."

"Who are your nurses? You still have Nancy?"

"Ya, Nancy's still working and I just hired two more." Bobby looked over at Charlie, who was sitting in the overstuffed chair, reading a magazine. "Charlie," he asked, "what are the names of the new nurses?"

"Janice Hallman is the new night shift nurse."

"Who's the other one?" Bobby asked.

"Didn't get a third one. She backed out. It seems the word's out that your house is haunted. Wally is telling everyone to stay away from here."

"Shit. Give Wally a call, will you? Ask him to stop spreading lies. You know what to say, right?" Bobby asked Charlie.

"I'm on it," said Charlie.

"Be sure you get another nurse, too. I want Bobby to have round-the-clock care when he starts using those crutches," Dr. Messenly told Charlie.

"Will do, Doc," Charlie said and left the bedroom.

"Did you hire a physical therapist yet?" the doctor asked Bobby.

"No. I didn't know I'd need one so soon."

"I've got a good one that would probably like to pick up a few bucks working an outside job. I'll ask him if he'd like to help out."

"Thanks. You leaving?"

"I've got rounds to make."

"What about the cast? And, the prescription?"

"I know, Bobby. Just get some rest. I'll take care of

it."

Charlie walked back into Bobby's room a few minutes after Dr. Messenly left.

"It's taken care of."

"What is?" Bobby asked.

"Both. I've got a new nurse. She'll work the night shift."

"What's her name?"

"Cynthia Bellman?"

"Get someone else."

"Why?" Charlie asked.

"I don't want anyone named Cynthia working here."

"Come on, Bobby. Be reasonable."

"Get someone else. What about Wally? What'd he say?"

"He understands that it is in his best interest to keep his big mouth shut."

"Good. Now call the agency back and tell them you need someone else."

"Good god, Bobby. You're drivin' me crazy."

"That's what you get paid for," Bobby said, laughing.

"Crazy wasn't part of the bargain," Charlie said.

"It's just a bonus, my friend," Bobby said, smiling. "Now go get that prescription filled. And, while you're at it, find out who's selling."

"What do you need more for? The doctor wrote you a pretty hefty prescription."

"Just in case. I figure a person should always have a backup plan. Now, get going, will you?"

Bobby heard the front door close, sighed, and closed his eyes. Cynthia, he thought. I can't even stand to hear that name spoken out loud.

She was such a dumb bitch, he thought. I never felt bad after I killed her. She deserved to die. I still can't believe those idiot cops bought the suicide thing. Of course, there was no reason not to. They just figured she couldn't face jail time for what she did to Sylvia and hung herself. Cynthia might not have been the one who actually pulled the trigger, but she set her up with that damn doctor and he went too far.

Why couldn't she have just accepted the fact that Big John was going to spend the rest of his life in jail? She couldn't keep her big nose out of it - obsessed to prove he was innocent. I didn't mind her fucking me, thinking she'd get me to talk. I used to wonder how far she'd go to prove that it was me, and not Big John, who killed my mother. I wish I'd known she was plotting to get Sylvia to recant her testimony against Big John, though. I coulda made that bitch disappear and Sylvia would still be alive.

I had a future with Sylvia. I loved her. She was probably the only woman I've actually, truly wanted to marry. Cynthia ruined that. Jail would have been way too good for that bitch.

I've been lucky, Bobby thought. More luck than brains, that's for sure. Well, I'm not ready for my luck to run out yet. It's time for Cal to join his wife in hell.

Chapter Fifteen

When Deputy George walked in the office, Sheriff Berkson was leaning back in his chair, feet up on his desk, enjoying his second cup of coffee. "Where you been?" he asked his deputy.

"Betsy called and asked me to come home. Lulu fell and hit her head. You know Betsy, panicking over every little thing."

"Is she okay?" the Sheriff inquired.

"She's fine. Just a little bump."

"Are you seriously gonna keep calling that little baby Lulu?"

"I guess. Betsy started calling her that from the beginning. Now, that's what everyone calls her."

"You know she's gonna be teased all her life, don't you?"

"Why's that? What's wrong with Lulu?" Casey asked.

"You never saw the cartoon strip, Little Lulu, in the funny papers?" the Sheriff asked him.

"Never heard of it," answered Casey.

"There was a TV show, some books, and a movie or two."

"Don't know it."

"Tubby was her fat little friend."

108

"Nope," said Casey.

"Well, I guess it's a generational thing. I just think you should be able to come up with a better nickname for Louisa than Lulu." He shrugged. "Hey, it's your kid. I'm sorry I brought it up. Call her whatever you want."

"Funtelli's back, Casey said, changing the subject. "He dropped off a bunch of fish. He said to take what you want."

"How's he doing?"

"Seriously, Cowboy, I don't think he's doing real well. He headed to Kansas City for the weekend. He said he'd be at work on Monday."

"He just came from that area. What does he think he's doing, going back up there?"

"You're not gonna like this," Casey said. "He decided to go see JoJo."

Sheriff Berkson took a sip of his coffee. He was quiet for a few seconds. "Damn that JoJo for coming back here. She's gonna break his heart all over again."

"He said he just wanted to ask her a few questions. Said he needed closure."

"Well, nothing I can do about it. Let's just hope he gets what he's looking for and can put this all behind him. Once again. Poor guy. You can't help but feel sorry for him," said the Sheriff.

"I'm going over to Minnie's Diner to get some donuts," said Casey. "Anything special I can bring you?"

"Naw. I promised Sarah I'd cut back on the sweets," the Sheriff replied.

"Be right back," said Casey, and headed for the door.

"Casey," the Sheriff yelled.

Casey turned and smiled at the Sheriff. "Jelly filled?" he asked.

At exactly 3:45 p.m., Simon Funtelli pulled into a parking space outside The McKenzie Institute in Kansas City, Missouri. He pulled down the visor and glanced in the mirror to see if his hair needed combing. He figured he looked okay and put the visor back in place. He reached for the door handle and then hesitated. Maybe Casey was right and I am being a fool, he thought. Do I really need to know what drove JoJo over the edge? Damned right I do, he decided and exited his car.

Five minutes later, he was led into an office and asked to take a seat. Someone would be with him shortly, he was told. Simon looked around the room and considered his surroundings. One word jumped out at him. Expensive. How could JoJo's parents afford this place? He didn't recall ever hearing that they had a lot of money.

He turned as the door opened and a distinguished-looking gentleman entered the room. The man shook Simon's hand. "Mr. Funtelli. I'm Dr. McKenzie. It's good to meet you."

"Likewise."

"I understand you'd like to visit JoJo Kirkham. I wished you had called before coming here. You made the trip for nothing, as, unfortunately, JoJo isn't allowed to have visitors."

"I don't understand," said Simon. "A week ago, she was at home visiting her parents. If she is well enough to visit her family, she should be able to see me."

"It's not that simple. We allowed JoJo to take her little furlough to see how she would handle it. As you know, it didn't go well. She managed to sneak out to a bar, where she came close to being killed. She can't be trusted. To be honest, Mr. Funtelli, I doubt very much that we will ever be able to trust her."

"I'd just like to talk to her for a few minutes," Simon said.

"I don't think that would be a good idea. Now, if you'll excuse me, I have things I need to attend to."

"Dr. McKenzie, I was going to ask JoJo to marry me. I loved her. Something happened to her and I don't know what it was. I need to know if it was something I did or, perhaps, didn't do. I know that JoJo isn't well, but she knows who I am. All I'm asking is for a few minutes. Please. I need this."

Dr. McKenzie looked at Simon. He shook his head back and forth, obviously still thinking that allowing Simon to visit with JoJo was a bad idea. "Let's sit for a minute," he said.

Simon sat down in a vintage high back chair. Dr. McKenzie sat across from him in the chair's matching companion. He was obviously considering how to approach this subject and didn't speak right away.

"Does JoJo remember that we were in love?" Simon asked, breaking the silence.

"You understand about doctor-patient confidentiality, don't you?"

"Of course," Simon replied.

"I can tell you this much. Three years ago, JoJo had a bad experience. She was probably fragile to begin with, so this affected her more than it would most women. I know you've been told by her parents that she tried to kill her boss, who was a minister."

"That's right," Simon said. "She was angry because he was piling so much work on her and wouldn't hire someone to help her. She was working

112

long hours without getting paid for the additional time. She mentioned a few times that she was going to quit."

"She remembers your relationship. She knows she loved you once. Believe me when I tell you that nothing you did caused her problems."

"Then, what did? What was the bad experience? I mean, what happened that was so horrible she couldn't tell me about it?"

"I'm sorry, Mr. Funtelli. I can't tell you."

"She had a bad experience . . ." Funtelli sat back in his chair. "More than most women, you said. Oh, my god. She was raped. That's it, isn't it? Someone raped her."

"I did not say that," said the doctor. "I did not tell you that. There is no basis for you to reach that conclusion."

"Who was it?" Funtelli yelled. He glared at the doctor. "Tell me, doctor. Who raped JoJo?"

"I'm sorry. This went too far. I'm going to ask you to leave now. The best thing you can do is just forget this conversation ever took place."

"Do you seriously think I'm going to forget this? A crime was committed against the woman I loved. And, it happened in my town, on my watch. No way, I'm gonna forget this. I promise you, someone is gonna pay for what they did to JoJo."

"Believe, Mr. Funtelli. It's better if you put it to rest. We made a big mistake by letting JoJo visit her parents. I can tell you, it will never happen again. Now, please leave."

"One more thing, Doctor. Who's paying for JoJo to be here? I know her parents don't have that kind of money. So, who's footing the bill?"

"I'm sorry you had a wasted trip, Mr. Funtelli. Please have a safe drive home."

Dr. McKenzie stood and walked to the door. He opened it and held it open, waiting for Funtelli to leave.

Simon started to say something but stopped himself. As he was leaving the room, he brushed up against Dr. McKenzie. He looked the doctor in the eyes, and said, "Thanks for your help, Doc. I know who did it."

Chapter Sixteen

"So, how was your trip?" the Sheriff asked Funtelli.

"Fine," he replied.

"Did you see JoJo?"

"Don't wanna talk about it," Funtelli told him.

"Thanks for the fish," the Sheriff said.

"Welcome," Funtelli said, and poured himself a cup of coffee.

"You want to talk?" the Sheriff asked him.

Funtelli turned and scowled at the Sheriff. "Do I look like I want to talk?"

Sheriff Berkson put his hands up. "Whoa, there. Just trying to help. Forget I said anything."

"Sorry. I kinda had a bad weekend. I didn't mean to snap like that."

Sheriff Berkson smiled. "Forget it. We all have our bad days. Are you ready to go over today's schedule?"

"Since when do we have a schedule?" Funtelli asked.

Sheriff Berkson eyeballed him, wondering if he was being a smart ass on purpose. "Seriously, Funtelli? You wanna start with me?

"No."

What do you think we do every morning? We go

over the schedule."

"I thought we called it an itinerary. Not important. How do I get into someone's bank records?"

Sheriff Berkson looked puzzled. "Why do you want to do that?"

"Is there a way without getting a court order?" Funtelli asked.

"Unless you know a good hacker, which I don't recommend, you'll need a court order."

"You think Brad could do it?" Funtelli asked, referring to Officer Brad Herzberg, the ITT Tech that worked for the Hollister Police Department.

"I know he could do it. I also know he won't do it. What's going on, Funtelli?"

"Nothing. I was just wondering," Funtelli answered.

"Simon?"

"Really. It's nothing. I was just wondering where the Kirkhams were getting the money to pay for JoJo's stay at that institution. You should see that place, Sheriff. It's like a friggin' palace. Someone's paying a fortune for her to be there. I just want to know who it is."

"Drop it, Simon. You haven't got cause to get a court order."

"I know that. I'm just curious, that's all."

"All right. Enough talk about JoJo and hacking computers. I want you to drive out to Bobby Johnson's place and check it out. I want to know if he still has someone walking around his property, carrying a gun. Maybe stop in and say 'hi'. Just tell him you were driving by and thought you'd stop and see how he's doing."

"You still figure something's going on out there?"

"I'm not sure. It was a quiet weekend, so maybe not. I'm not closing the case on the boat accident yet. I'm gonna give it a few more weeks."

"You want me to stop on my way back and pick up a dozen donuts?"

"Absolutely not," replied the Sheriff. "I'm off sweets."

Deputy Casey George, who had just come in, looked at Fratelli. "Morning. Did I hear someone mention donuts?"

"Yep. I was gonna pick up a dozen, but Sheriff said I can't. Says he's off sweets."

"Well, I'm not. Either are the rest of the guys. The Sheriff may not want one, but I sure do."

"No more donuts in this office," said the Sheriff. "That's an order."

117

Funtelli smiled and walked towards the door. "You like any favorite kind, Sheriff?" he asked.

"No donuts," he replied. "I mean it."

"Doesn't make any difference what you get. He likes all of them," said Casey, laughing.

"Are you two deaf?" the Sheriff yelled, as Funtelli walked out.

"You don't have to eat them, you know," Casey told him.

Bobby Johnson had enjoyed a peaceful weekend. He was more alert being off the pain shots and he was not sleeping as much.

He glanced over at the clock on his nightstand. It was only eight-thirty. He was waiting for the physical therapist, who was scheduled to arrive around ten. His first session was to include being shown how to walk with crutches. He didn't quite understand why you had to be shown how to use crutches. It seemed pretty self-explanatory to him. But the doctor had insisted that he be instructed by the physical therapist. Besides, the doctor had said, the crutches have to be set to the exact height for maximum comfort, and it was best if the physical therapist did that.

Whatever the doctor wanted, he was gonna agree

to. He couldn't wait to get out of bed, even if it was just to go to the bathroom.

He looked over at Nancy, his nurse, who was sitting in the overstuffed chair reading a magazine.

"How about propping up my pillows?" he asked her. "I'd like to be able to see out the window."

"Sure thing, Bobby," she said.

As she rose from the chair, Bobby heard a pop pop pop sound from outside. His bedroom window shattered and there was a thud next to him. He glanced back at his headboard and saw that the wood had been splintered by a bullet.

"What the hell is . . ." He stopped talking when he saw the look on Nancy's face. She was touching her right shoulder with her left hand. When she pulled her hand away, it was covered with blood.

"Charlie," Bobby screamed. "Get it here. Nancy's been shot."

John Luke, who heard the shot from where he was patrolling in the backyard, ran into Bobby's room, yelling for everyone to stay down.

"Nancy's been shot. Call 911," Bobby yelled.

John Luke looked at Nancy and saw that her face was almost white. Taking her arm, he gently lowered her into the chair. He ran into the bathroom and grabbed a towel. "Hold this against your shoulder," he told her. Then, he called for an ambulance.

"Where's Charlie?" Bobby asked John Luke.

"He's in the pool. I'll get him."

"I'm here," said Charlie, as he ran into the room, water dripping from his body. "I thought I heard shots. What the hell happened here?"

"Someone shot at us," Bobby said. "The shots came from the road and straight through the window. One hit Nancy. One just missed me. It's in the headboard."

"I thought I heard three shots," Charlie said. "Have you called for an ambulance?"

"Done," replied John Luke.

"Where were you?" Bobby asked John Luke.

"Checking the back of the house. I'm telling you, Bobby, we need two people guarding the outside of the house instead of just one. One person can't be everywhere. Damn! This really pisses me off."

"How you doin' there, Nancy?" Bobby asked.

"Hurts like hell, Bobby. How do ya think I'm doing?"

"Hang in there, girl. Help should be here any minute now."

"Did you see the car?" Charlie asked Bobby.

"No. But, it sounded more like a truck than a car."

"I hear sirens. Looks like the paramedics are here," said Charlie.

At the same time the ambulance pulled into Bobby's driveway, Officer Funtelli arrived at Bobby's house. Funtelli stopped his car across the street from Bobby's house and turned off the engine. He watched as the paramedics ran to the front door and entered the house. A few minutes later, one of the paramedics came out and opened the rear of the ambulance. Then, the second paramedic exited the house and helped his partner carry a stretcher into the house.

Funtelli got out of his car, walked across the road, and entered Bobby's house. He heard a commotion going on in Bobby's bedroom, walked over to the door, and looked in. The paramedics were working on a woman's shoulder.

"Hey, Bobby," he said. "What's going on here?"

Bobby jumped. "Fuck, Funtelli. You scared the shit out of me. How long have you been standing there?"

"Just got here. I was driving by and saw the ambulance. I thought I'd stop and see what was going on. What happened here?"

"My nurse got hurt. Nothing to worry about. It's all under control," Bobby told him"

121

One of the paramedics glanced over at Funtelli. "She was shot, Officer."

Funtelli exchanged looks with Bobby. "Who shot her, Bobby?" he asked.

Bobby looked away. "I honestly have no idea. The shots came from outside. Maybe someone was hunting in the woods across the street. It might have been a stray bullet."

"Hunting what? You said shots. Was there more than one shot?" Funtelli asked.

Nancy glanced over at Funtelli. "I heard three shots," she said quietly.

"Squirrels are. And, groundhogs," said Bobby.

"What?" Funtelli asked.

"In season. You wanted to know what someone could be hunting," Bobby replied.

Funtelli watched as the paramedics loaded Nancy onto the stretcher and wheeled her out of the room. Funtelli followed them to their ambulance and waited until Nancy was placed into the back of the vehicle.

"Did anyone mention who they thought might have done the shooting?" Funtelli asked the driver of the ambulance.

"Not while I was in there," he replied. "Sorry, but we gotta go."

Funtelli watched as the ambulance drove off, sirens blaring. He took his phone out of his pocket and hit number two on speed dial.

"What's up, Funtelli?" Sheriff Berkson said.

"There's been a shooting up here at Bobby's."

"Shit! Anybody hurt?"

"His nurse got hit in the shoulder. She'll be okay. One of the bullets just missed Bobby. You want to get over here or should I handle it?" Funtelli asked.

"Who did the shooting?"

"Don't know. It looks like a drive-by."

"I'll be there in a few minutes. Are you in the house?"

"I'm outside."

"Get in there and keep an eye on everyone until I get there. Don't let anyone leave. What was the nurse's name?"

"Nancy something. Didn't get her last name. She's on her way to the hospital right now."

"Okay. I'll send Casey over to get her statement. Was it a through and through or is the bullet still in her shoulder?"

"I'm not sure, Sheriff."

"I'll have Casey find out. If it's not in her shoulder, we'll need to find it."

"I'll dig out the shot that hit Bobby's headboard and bag it," Funtelli told the Sheriff. "Nancy said she heard three shots. I don't know where the third shot hit. We'll have to look around for it."

"Remember, you're dealing with a crime scene, Funtelli."

"I know, Sheriff."

"I'm on my way."

Chapter Seventeen

Officer Funtelli was pacing back and forth in front of the table that held the coffee server and cups. Sheriff Berkson glanced up from his desk. "You're irritating the crap out of me, Funtelli. Either stop that pacing and sit down or get the hell out of here for a while."

Funtelli stopped and looked at the Sheriff in surprise. "Did you say something, Sheriff?"

"Stop that damn pacing, will you?"

"Sorry. It's just that I'm so friggin' frustrated. I think I know who's picking up JoJo's tab at that high and mighty clinic she's in, but I can't prove it."

"What difference does it make?" asked the Sheriff. "Why are you so obsessed with this?"

Funtelli pulled up a chair and sat down across from his boss, a serious look on his face. "I figure whoever is paying is the same person who hurt her. It's blood money, so to speak."

"Why don't you just ask JoJo's parents where the money's coming from?" the Sheriff questioned. Then, it dawned on him what Funtelli had just said. He looked questioningly at Funtelli. "What do you mean hurt JoJo? I thought she just had a breakdown and went off the handle."

"Promise you won't repeat this, Sheriff?" Funtelli

asked.

"I guess."

"No guesses. You promise?"

"Of course. I promise I won't repeat what you're about to tell me."

"JoJo was raped. That's why she went 'off the handle' as you put it."

Sheriff Berkson leaned back in his chair and frowned at Funtelli. "Just how do you know this?" he asked.

"That doctor, McKenzie, told me. Well, he didn't come right out and say it, but it was implied. When I pushed him on the subject, he clammed up and said he never said it. But that's what happened. I know it. It all makes sense now. JoJo suddenly complaining about being stressed out and not being able to sleep. Then, she wants to quit her job. But, what does she do? She takes a gun to her boss' house – who's a minister for crying out loud - and tries to kill him. It had to be him who raped her. Why else would she want him dead? That's why I need to find out who's footing the bill. I need to be sure."

"Whoa. Slow down, Simon. I'm sorry about what happened to JoJo. If, it actually did happen. But you don't know for sure if it did, and you can't just hack into

126

people's bank records. Did you ever consider that JoJo's parents borrowed the money or maybe someone is helping them out?"

"Of course, I have. I've gone over everything in my head a million times. I don't think it's coming from JoJo's parents. I think somebody agreed to pay the fee to the McKenzie Institution so that her parents would keep their mouths shut. I just can't prove it. Yet."

"Well, let's go back to my original question. Why don't you just ask her parents where the money is coming from?" the Sheriff said.

"I did," Funtelli said.

"You talked to them?" the Sheriff asked, surprised.

"I did. And, they wouldn't say anything. They told me that I was way off base if I thought that JoJo had been raped. They said I should keep my big nose out of their business."

"That would probably be best, Simon," the Sheriff quietly commented. "You're upset and with good reason. JoJo shows up after being missing for three years. Obviously, you need answers but fabricating a story isn't going to help. It's only going to hurt you more."

Funtelli gave the Sheriff a dirty look. "You think I made this story up in my mind?"

"I'm not saying that, Simon. It's just that you have nothing to go on. Look at you. You're a wreck, pacing the floor, and not concentrating on your job. You've got to stop this before you drive yourself crazy."

Funtelli sat back in his chair and stared at the Sheriff. After a few awkward seconds, he let out a deep sigh. "You're right. I don't know what actually happened to JoJo and I am driving myself nuts over this. I'm sorry I've been distracted. I'll try to get back on track."

"I know it's hard, Simon," Sheriff Berkson said. "I'm here for you if you need to talk or – well, if you need anything. Just let me know if there's something I can do."

Officer Funtelli stood up and smiled at the Sheriff. "You're a good friend, Cowboy. Thanks for listening. Guess I better get my ass back to work."

Deputy George was glancing down at a piece of paper he was carrying, as he walked in from the back room of the police station. "Forensics sent over the report on the bullet we dug out of Bobby Johnson's headboard. It matches the one that was removed from Nancy Carson's shoulder," he said.

When no one acknowledged his comment, he looked up. "Sorry, did I interrupt something?" he asked.

Funtelli shook his head no, and walked over to his

desk, and sat down. Sheriff Berkson looked up at Casey. "What does the report say, Casey," he asked.

Casey exchanged looks with the Sheriff. "Everything okay here?"

"Of course," Berkson replied. "What kind of gun are we looking for?"

"A .45. What else would it be? Everyone and their uncle own a .45. Trying to find the person who owns that gun is going to be like looking for a needle in a haystack."

"Not if we narrow it down to just a few," the Sheriff said.

"Like who?" Casey asked.

"Well, for one, we can start with Cal Cuddihey. Find out if he has a .45."

"Who else?" Casey inquired.

The Sheriff didn't say anything, obviously thinking about Casey's question. He looked up at Casey and shook his head. "Crap, Casey. I can't think of anyone else."

Chapter Eighteen

Officer Funtelli's body jerked as he woke up. He rubbed his eyes and wiped a small amount of dribble off his chin with the back of his hand. He glanced at his watch and swore. It was almost eleven o'clock. He looked across the street and saw that the inside of the church was dark. Funtelli had planned on confronting Pastor McCarthy after the pastor finished teaching an adult bible study group. The cars that had been parked in the church's parking lot were gone. Too late now, Funtelli thought as he started his car and pulled out of his parking spot.

As he started to drive by the church, he saw a person walking in the parking lot. He hit his brakes and stared. The man had crossed the lot and was headed towards the parsonage, which was next to the church. Funtelli backed the car up, then shifted into drive, and drove into the driveway that led to the back of the church.

The man stopped walking and watched as Funtelli's car approached him. Funtelli stopped his car, put it in park, and got out. "Is that you, Pastor?" he yelled.

"It is. Is there something I can do for you?"

"I was just driving by. I didn't know it was you, so

I thought I'd just check to make sure everything's okay."

Pastor McCarthy took a few steps towards Funtelli. "I was just finishing up some paperwork. Everything is fine. Officer Frantulli, is it?"

"Close. It's Funtelli."

"Sorry. I'm terrible with names," Pastor McCarthy said.

"You got a few minutes?" Funtelli asked. "I'd like to ask you a couple of questions."

"It's kinda late and I was planning to go to bed. Is it something that can wait until tomorrow?"

"It won't take long, Pastor. Why don't we just talk in my car for a few minutes?"

Pastor McCarthy glanced around at his surroundings. "Well, I guess I can spare a few minutes." He walked to the passenger side of Funtelli's car, got in, and watched as Funtelli sat down in the driver's seat. "So, what can I help you with, Officer?"

"Did you know that JoJo was in town last week?" Funtelli asked him.

Pastor McCarthy's head jerked up in surprise. "I didn't know that."

"Yep. She's alive. She's not dead like we all thought for the past three years. No sir, Pastor. She's alive and kicking and more than just a little crazy. But you know that, don't you? You helped make the arrangements for her to be put in that institution. You and her parents. You raped her and drove her nuts. And, now, you're paying the cost of keeping her locked up in that nut house, so her parents will keep quiet."

Pastor McCarthy stared at him. "What in the world are you talking about? Raped her? I wasn't the one who raped her."

"I knew it. I knew she was raped. If you didn't do it, then why did she try to shoot you?"

Pastor McCarthy turned his head away from Funtelli and looked out the window. "I can't tell you," he finally said.

"Here's the deal. You tell me what happened with JoJo and I don't arrest you for obstruction of justice. Rape is a crime, even if it isn't reported to the authorities. You knew about a crime and you hid it. I want the whole story and I want to hear it now. You're not getting out of this car until you tell me what I want to know."

Pastor McCarthy shook his head no. "I can't. I promised JoJo's parents that it would stay between us."

"Not good enough, Pastor. Tell me what you promised would stay between you and the Kirkhams."

Pastor McCarthy put his hand on the door handle.

"I'm sorry, Mr. Funtelli, I can't"

Funtelli reached for his arm to keep him from leaving the car. When he saw the frightened look on Pastor McCarthy's face, he stopped. "I'm sorry, but I need answers. I just about went crazy after losing JoJo. I figured she was dead. Almost everyone thought she was dead. Except, you knew better. So, did her parents. I don't get it. Why hide the fact that she was still alive? Why the big cover-up? She tried to shoot you. If you weren't the one who raped her, then why'd she try to kill you? Why not the person who actually did it? None of this makes sense."

"Not everything has to make sense. . ."

Funtelli interrupted him. "And, who's paying for her to stay in that expensive institution? Dr. McKenzie said she'll probably be there for the rest of her life. Just who is it, Pastor, if it isn't you?"

"I can't tell you. If I tell you, her funding stops and she'll be placed in a county-run hospital. Have you ever seen what goes on in those places?"

Funtelli took a deep breath, trying to control his anger. "I'm not letting this go. I don't give a tinker's damn if you are a minister. You're not Catholic and you can't claim that you'd be breaking the seal of confession."

"I promised. I can't go against my word. It would be a sin if I did. So, I think we're done here and I'd like to go home."

"Tell me what happened to JoJo. You don't have to give me a name," Funtelli said. "Just tell me and then you can go home to your nice soft bed and sleep your 'oh, I'm so innocent' sleep."

Pastor McCarthy closed his eyes, thinking about the night that JoJo appeared on his doorstep, holding that gun. He knew how frustrated Mr. Funtelli was, and knew that he wasn't going to let up asking questions. Finally, he looked over at Funtelli and said, "She didn't try to kill me. She tried to kill my wife."

Chapter Nineteen

Just as Cal Cuddihey made a move towards Officer George, Officer Funtelli stepped between them. Cuddihey stopped, looked up at Funtelli, and took a step back.

"You better rethink your attitude, Cal," Funtelli said. "I'd love nothing better than to punch your lights out right now."

"Whoa, Big Guy," Cuddihey said. "Take it easy. I'm good." He looked at Casey, put his hands up, and smiled. "Take the damn gun. You're way off base, thinking I shot someone. Go ahead, take it. Just make sure I get it back when you're done making a fool of yourself."

Casey deposited the gun into an evidence bag and sealed it. "Let's go Funtelli," he said, as he walked towards his squad car. He turned and looked back at Cuddihey, who was glaring at him. "Just be sure you don't leave town, Cal."

Cuddihey's face turned red. He started to move towards the Deputy, thought better of it, and stopped.

As Funtelli headed towards the car, he walked past Cuddihey, gave him a shove with his shoulder, and threw Cuddihey off balance.

"What the fuck, Funtelli!" Cuddihey yelled.

135

Funtelli quit walking, turned, and glared at Cuddihey. "You want to say something?" he asked, threatening.

Cuddihey stared back at Funtelli, spit on the ground, turned, and walked back to his house.

Casey was quiet as he started driving down the hilly road towards town. After a few minutes, he looked over at Funtelli and asked, "What the hell was that all about?"

"What?" Funtelli snapped.

"That scene back there. You were egging him on – just looking for a fight."

"He pissed me off. Okay? I'm tired of getting attitude from everybody. We're here to help people and all we get is attitude. Like, we're the bad guys. I'm fucking tired of it all. Okay?"

Casey glanced at him and didn't respond. Something was up with him and Casey decided it was better not to pursue it right now. He had known Funtelli for years and this was the first time he had seen him act like this. And, he didn't like what he was seeing.

Casey pulled into the back of the Police Station and parked his vehicle. He looked over at Funtelli, who had been quiet on the rest of the drive back to town.

"You coming in?" he asked Funtelli, as they got out of the car.

"Nope. I'm gonna go do some patrolling. Maybe, catch me a few speeders. Call me if the Sheriff needs me." He walked over to his squad car, started it up, and pulled away.

Man, Casey thought, as he walked towards the back door of the station, something is really biting his ass.

Funtelli drove out of Hollister on Hwy. 76, and turned onto Lake Shore Drive. He drove up the hilly road until he found a spot, overlooking Lake Taneycomo, where he could park his car. He needed to get away from everything and think. He didn't know how to process the information that Pastor McCarthy had told him the night before.

He had dated JoJo for a long time, yet he never saw any signs that she was so mentally unstable. He found it hard to accept that everything Pastor McCarthy told him was true, yet he believed that he had told him the truth.

He was in a dilemma. If he killed Bobby Johnson, JoJo's funding would stop. If he didn't kill him, Bobby Johnson would get away with rape.

137

Pastor McCarthy had said he wasn't one hundred percent sure that JoJo had actually been raped. JoJo said she had, but the story she told the pastor sounded more like she got drunk and consented to have sex with Bobby Johnson. Then, guilt set in, and her story changed.

Funtelli tried to think back and remember a night that JoJo had gone out partying with her friends. He couldn't remember one in particular, but the time factor coincided with when her personality started to change. She had become distant and moody. She canceled dates with him, and became less affectionate, taking sex off the table. He had planned on asking her to marry him, but he held off, waiting for her to get over whatever was bothering her. When he would ask her what was wrong, she'd say everything was fine and it was just his imagination.

He had listened to Pastor McCarthy without interrupting him. He had a million questions he wanted to ask him, but he had kept quiet until the minister finished talking.

"JoJo went out partying with some of her girlfriends," the pastor told Funtelli. "They hooked up with Bobby Johnson and a few of his friends at some bar.

I don't remember which one. It seems that most of them were wasted and they decided it would be a good idea to go swimming in Bobby's pool. After more drinking at Bobby's house, the clothes came off and everyone wound up skinny dipping. JoJo hooked up with Bobby. They started making out, but when it went too far, JoJo tried to stop it. She said she told him no, but he ignored her. She'd had a lot to drink, couldn't fight him off, and they had sex. Was it rape, Mr. Funtelli? Who knows? It's a she said/he said situation. Personally, I think it was consensual. But the guilt started creeping in and she cried rape."

Pastor McCarthy stopped talking. He studied Funtelli's face for a couple of seconds. "You want me to continue?"

Funtelli shook his head yes.

"The next day at work, she broke down crying. She told me what had happened and begged me not to tell anyone. I comforted her. I told her that God would always love her, no matter what happened. She didn't seem to get better over the next few days. She was constantly crying and I was doing my best to help her."

"She threw herself into her work, often working hours past closing time. Gradually, she started to settle down and it seemed she was pulling herself together.

139

Then, one day, right out of the blue, she told me that she no longer loved you. I'm sorry, Mr. Funtelli, but you wanted to hear it all. She agonized over getting up the nerve to tell you that she wanted to end your relationship. She never told you, did she?"

Funtelli answered, softly saying, "No."

The pastor continued. "I thought she was getting better. You know, she wasn't crying as much, and she started smiling again. I even heard her humming at her desk. One night, as she was getting ready to leave, I gave her a little hug – like always - and she kissed me hard on the lips. I backed away and told her that it was not appropriate for her to do that. She started to cry and told me that she was sorry. She said that she had fallen in love with me."

Pastor McCarthy stopped talking. He took a deep breath and let it out.

"I'm sorry. This is hard for me, too." He paused for a few seconds, and then he continued telling Funtelli what had happened. "After that night, she continued to confess her love for me. She told me she wanted me to divorce my wife and marry her. I explained to her that I loved my wife and I would never divorce her. I told her that, as much as I would hate losing her, I wanted her to find a new job. I couldn't have her working for me any
140

longer. *She was putting my marriage and my job in jeopardy. She told me she was sorry, that she understood, and she would look for a position somewhere else."*

"It wasn't long after that – less than a week, I would guess - she was standing on my porch, ringing the doorbell. You have no idea how much I wish my wife had not answered the door, Mr. Funtelli. JoJo was standing there, pointing a gun at her. She pulled the trigger. If that gun had been loaded, my wife would be dead now."

"I got the gun away from JoJo and calmed her down. We called JoJo's parents and told them to come over. My wife didn't want to press charges. It was obvious that JoJo was sick and we didn't want to have her arrested and end up in jail. After a lengthy discussion with her parents, about what had been going on, we decided to get her the help she needed. There was no point in waiting to see if she'd get better. I called my friend, Dr. McKenzie, and asked if there was a room available for JoJo. He agreed to take her in. The only drawback was money. As you found out, the McKenzie Institute is very expensive."

"We called Bobby Johnson. Basically, we blackmailed him into paying for her care at the Institute for as long as it was needed. We told him it was either

141

that or JoJo would accuse him of raping her. He agreed. Her parents packed a suitcase and drove her to Kansas City. She's been there ever since. I didn't know, until you told me, that she was well enough to come back for a visit."

"She wasn't," Funtelli replied. "Dr. McKenzie used bad judgment there. JoJo actually thinks she's engaged to him. She isn't any better."

"I'm sorry to hear that," said Pastor McCarthy.

"One question, Pastor."

"Of course."

"Why did you let everyone think that JoJo was missing or maybe even dead? Why couldn't you just tell people she'd had a breakdown? Or, that she had decided to take a long vacation? Anything at all, except that. Look at all the time and money that was spent looking for her. And, for what reason?" Funtelli asked.

"It seems silly now, doesn't it? But it was what we agreed to at the time. None of us were thinking clearly. We decided that no one was to tell. I think it might have been Bobby Johnson who put in that stipulation. Believe me, if I had it to do over, I would do it differently. However, the Kirkhams didn't want anyone to know their daughter tried to kill my wife and that she had a breakdown. So, maybe it was their idea. It's not

142

important now, is it?"

Pastor McCarthy had looked at Funtelli, waiting for his response. Funtelli held the pastor's gaze until the pastor looked away. "Not if you don't care that someone was raped, it's not," Funtelli finally said. "Now, get out of my car."

Pastor McCarthy started to say something, hesitated, opened the car door, and got out of the car. As he was about to close the door, he said, "I'm sorry. I really am."

"Not good enough, Pastor. Too little, too late. As for you, your wife, and the Kirkhams – well, I hope you all rot in hell."

Funtelli heaved a deep sigh, opened his car door, got out, and walked over to the edge of the cliff. He looked down at the water. It's my fault, he thought. How did I not see her deterioration? I should have helped her. I figured she'd just get over whatever was bugging her.

She was drunk. If she didn't know what she was doing, it was rape. She was raped by Bobby Johnson and I want that fucking bastard dead.

Funtelli walked back to his car and sat sideways on the seat, his feet on the ground. He glanced up at a white cloud, floating across the blue sky, and watched its shape change as the wind carried it along. Finally, he started his car. As he put it in reverse, he looked up at the cloud one more time and shuddered. He swore the cloud had just metamorphosed into the face of the devil.

<u>Chapter Twenty</u>

"Man, was he pissed off," Casey said.

"Tough."

"For a minute or two I thought he was gonna take a swing at me."

"So, he's got a temper, does he?" asked Sheriff Berkson.

"I'd say so. A really short fuse. The minute I asked him if he owned a .45, he got defensive. When I told him I needed to take it, he got pissed off. He said no way was he givin' up his gun. When I showed him the court order, he came at me."

"What stopped him?"

"I took Funtelli with me. The minute Cal took a step towards me, Funtelli stepped between us. You know there ain't nobody gonna mess with him."

Sheriff Berkson laughed. "He can be scary at times."

"I think Funtelli's having a bad day."

"How so?" asked the Sheriff.

"He got pretty aggressive with Cal."

"He's having a bad time getting over this JoJo thing. He'll be okay. He just needs to sort some things out. So, Cal gave you the gun?"

"It's being checked now," answered Casey. "We'll

know in a little while if it's the gun that was used to shoot Nancy Carson."

"How many guns did you find?"

"He had a few more handguns, a shotgun, two rifles, and his archery equipment."

"You ever go bow and arrow hunting, Casey?" the Sheriff asked.

"Never got the hang of it. It takes a special talent to use that stuff," replied Casey.

"He could have more than one .45. He might have gotten rid of the gun, you know," the Sheriff commented.

"Or, he might have hid it someplace," Casey said.

"How long before we get the report?"

"Forensics said we'd have it within an hour or so. Let's just keep our fingers crossed on this one," Casey replied.

"Ya," said the Sheriff. "That always works."

Bobby had asked his nurse to take a walk outside, so he could have some privacy. He was sitting in a chair in the living room, his bad leg resting on a footstool.

Bobby watched as Charlie, John Luke, and Sammy tried to make up their minds as to which chairs they wanted to sit on. The Three Stooges, Bobby thought. Dear lord, help me. I'm dealing with a bunch of idiots.

"Sit down!" he yelled.

The three men looked surprised, quickly picked a chair, and sat down.

"What's biting your butt," Charlie asked.

"Are you all comfortable?" Bobby sarcastically asked, and watched while they shook their heads yes.

"Good. We need to talk and this is in strict confidence. None of you can repeat this. Understand?"

Again, all three shook their heads in agreement.

"I need a hit man. Cal Cuddihey has to go away. I'd do it myself if I could but, obviously, that's not an option."

"Why's he trying to kill you?" John Luke asked.

"You don't need to know. In fact, the less you know, the better," replied Bobby

John Luke looked over at Charlie. "Do you know, Charlie?" he asked.

"Haven't got a clue," Charlie lied. "But, if Bobby says he's got to go, that's good enough for me."

"What's the job pay?" asked Charlie.

"It depends," replied Bobby.

"How about Phil Wilson? He's doing a good job here and he needs the money," suggested John Luke.

"No. I don't want anyone from town. I need

someone who can sneak in and out of here and never be seen again. Maybe from Chicago or St. Louis. I don't care from where, but not from here."

The room was quiet for a few minutes. Finally, Sammy spoke up. "I know someone. But it will cost you."

"How much?" Bobby asked.

"At least fifty big ones."

"Is he good?"

Sammy glanced over at John Luke and Charlie. "Maybe, it would be best if they didn't hear this."

"You two. Give us a few minutes. Go take a walk."

Sammy waited until Charlie and John Luke shut the front door. "It's not a he. It's a she."

"A woman hitman?"

"I guess you could call her a hitwoman."

"Whatever. Who is she?"

"Alicia."

"Your wife?" Bobby exclaimed. "What the fuck you telling me, Sammy. Alicia wouldn't hurt a fly."

"You're right. But, for fifty thousand dollars, she'd kill her own grandmother."

Bobby stared at him in disbelief. "I can't wrap my head around this. How long has she been doing this?"

"Let's just say she earned her bones a long time

148

ago, when she was living in St. Louis. That's where we met, you know. Remember, I was up there years ago doing that construction job?"

"I remember," said Bobby. "You came back married to her."

"She's good, Bobby. She only does a few jobs a year now. You know, with the twins and all, it's hard to get away without anyone getting suspicious. The extra money is nice. I can ask her if you want."

"I can't have anyone who can be connected back to me," Bobby said. "What if she gets caught? The cops will know it was me that hired her."

"She won't get caught. I can promise you that. Why don't I call her and see what she says? You can get an answer right now."

Bobby hesitated before answering him. "All right. Call her."

Sammy took his cell phone out of his back pocket and headed for the kitchen. "I'll be right back," he told Bobby.

Bobby stared out the window overlooking his backyard. His swimming pool looked so inviting. He would give anything to be able to just jump in and do some laps. Damn leg, he thought. Cal sure has screwed up my life.

He looked questioningly at Sammy, as he walked back into the living room. Sammy shook his head no.

"She won't do it?" Bobby asked him.

"No. She asked that you don't take offense to her refusal to help you out, but she said to tell you that she – and I'm quoting here, Bobby – she 'doesn't shit where she eats'."

Bobby laughed. "Smart lady, Sammy. It was a bad idea, anyway."

"However, she did say that she might know someone. She's gonna check it out and let me know. Hopefully, by tonight if she can get ahold of the guy."

"Good. You want to tell John Luke and Charlie to come back in?"

"What about the nurse. Janice? Right?"

"Ya. Tell her she can come in. Actually, just tell Charlie and her to come in. John Luke and you can get back to work."

"It's a hot one out there today," Sammy commented.

"Just drink a lot of water. If we're lucky and find someone to do the job, this patrolling crap will end soon."

"Sorry, I couldn't help you," Sammy said.

"Hey, don't worry about it. Things will work out.

I'll tell you something, though. I'll never look at Alicia the same way. You have yourself one hell of a woman there."

Sammy smiled. "I sure do, Bobby. They broke the mold when they made her."

"Okay, then. You want to get Charlie back in here?"

"I'm on it," Sammy said.

A few minutes later, Charlie came back into the house and sat down across from Bobby.

"I'm tired of watching my back, Charlie. This has to end now. You want the job?"

Charlie stared at him. "Bobby, you know I've never killed anybody. I don't know if I could do it."

"One hundred thousand. That's what I'll give you if you figure out a way to get rid of Cuddihey and not get caught."

Charlie sat back in his chair, obviously unnerved. He shook his head from side to side. "That's a lot of money, Bobby."

"There's a lot of ways to kill someone, Charlie. It's not that hard if you figure out the right way."

Charlie stood up, walked to the window overlooking the pool, and gazed out. Bobby stayed quiet, letting Charlie think about his proposal. Finally, Charlie turned and locked eyes with Bobby.

"I'll do it," he said, emphatically. "For you, I'll do it."

Chapter Twenty-one

"It sure has been quiet around here," Casey said, as he opened another packet of sugar.

"You're gonna get fat or something even worse if you keep putting all that sugar in your coffee. What is that? The third one?" asked the Sheriff.

"What can I say? I like it sweet," Casey replied.

Sheriff Berkson and Deputy George were sitting in Minnie's Diner, discussing the lack of activity for the past six days. The traffic stops were down, there had only been a few nuisance calls, and no funeral processions to help direct to a cemetery.

"Have you come up with any more suspects in the Johnson shooting?" Casey asked.

"Nope," replied the Sheriff. "Cuddihey was the only one I could come up with. Even though I think he tried to kill Bobby and probably did kill Katie, I can't prove it. His gun was clean and Bobby still isn't talking."

"You think Bobby had an affair with Katie, Sheriff?"

"I do. I think Cuddihey found out about it and tried to kill 'em all by driving the boat into that dock."

"Well," commented Casey, "if that was his goal, he sure as hell didn't do a very good job. I could think of a lot of other ways to get revenge. Three bullets would

153

have done the job."

"Anger does funny things to people, Casey. There's no telling what someone is capable of."

"I just hope that's the end of it with him and Bobby. It's nice to have peace and quiet again."

Sheriff Berkson frowned. "I have a feeling that we haven't heard the end of it, yet. You know what they say about trouble. It always comes in threes."

Casey looked up and glanced at the Sheriff. "Well, that's a doom and gloom attitude."

"Well, just remember this, Casey. Things never get so bad that they can't get worse."

"How do you think Funtelli is doing?" Casey asked, changing the subject.

"He seems okay. I guess he's accepting the JoJo thing. That was a lot to swallow all at once."

"Yea, he'll be fine. He sure has been quiet, though," Casey said.

"He never has been much of a talker," the Sheriff said. "Thank goodness," he added, laughing.

"Wish he'd find himself a nice girl and settle down," Casey remarked.

"He will. Just has to find the right one. Phone," he said, as he picked his phone up off the table, and answered a call.

"What's up?" he asked Officer Tim Carlson.

Casey watched as the Sheriff frowned. The Sheriff ended the call, threw some money on the table, and grabbed his hat. "Let's go," he said. "Bad car accident out by the bridge."

Bobby hobbled into the kitchen. Charlie was sitting at the table, totally absorbed in what he was doing.

"Whatcha doing there, Charlie?" Bobby asked playfully.

Charlie jumped. "Good god, Bobby," he exclaimed. "You gotta quit creeping up on people. You scared the crap out of me?"

Bobby laughed. "Hell, Charlie. Your nerves are shot. So, just what are you doing?"

"I'm building a bomb. Gonna blow Cal to smithereens."

Bobby looked at the items Charlie had on top of the kitchen table. He saw batteries, some wire, a toggle switch, a soldering gun, wire cutters, screwdrivers, plus numerous items he wasn't familiar with. "What are you gonna use the toggle switch for?" he asked, grinning.

Charlie looked confused. "I'm not sure. I read somewhere that I would need one. I'm still collecting

155

stuff."

Bobby smiled from ear to ear. "You're an idiot, Charlie. You'll never be able to build a bomb." He laughed. "What are you using for the explosive?" Bobby asked.

"I've got to get some C-4 plastic. Do you have any idea where I can get that?" Charlie asked.

"No. What are you going to tell Karen if she walks in here? You gonna tell her that you're building a bomb so you can blow Cal Cuddihey to pieces?"

"She went to Springfield. Some family thing."

"She didn't ask me if she could have time off."

"You were sleeping, so she asked me. I told her she could take the whole day. I don't think we need more than one nurse, anyway," Charlie told him. "Maybe just during the day would be enough. I'm here nights if you need anything. Why don't you let one go?"

"I'll think about it."

Bobby pulled a chair out away from the table and sat down. He used both hands to lift his bad leg and place it on another chair. "Charlie, I think we should find someone else. I don't think you're up to this. You can't build a bomb here in my kitchen. What the hell you gonna say if someone shows up? This is supposed to be between you and me." He hesitated as he looked at

156

the items on the table again. "Do you even know what you're doing?"

Charlie shook his head. "You're right," he said. "I don't know what the hell I'm doing. Maybe you should find someone else."

"Or, you can do it the easy way."

Charlie looked over at him. "What do you mean? The easy way?"

"First, you need to get a gun that can't be traced. That's easy enough. There're enough of them available in Springfield. Better yet, drive up to St. Louis and get one. Then, hide in the woods near Cal's house and wait for him to leave. A few well-aimed shots should take him out."

"What if he sees my truck parked on the road?"

Bobby stared at him. "Seriously? Let's just call this off, Charlie. I really don't think you have it in you."

"You're right. I shouldn't have volunteered. It's just that the money was tempting."

"All right, then. Gather up all this crap on the table and dump it. And, not in my garbage. Go throw it in the lake or something. Just get it out of here," Bobby told him.

"Sorry, Bobby," Charlie said.

"Nothing to be sorry about. Sammy's still looking

157

for someone. He's gonna let me know if any of his leads pan out. Anyway, it's been quiet for almost a week now. Maybe Cal has had a change of heart."

"Maybe," said Charlie. "But, if I know Cal, as well as I think I do, he's busy planning his next move."

<u>Chapter Twenty-two</u>

The last car was being towed away. The piercing wail of the ambulance's siren could still be heard as it headed towards Branson Community Hospital. Since the roundabout, which was on the Hollister side of the bridge, had been completed, the number of accidents in that location had risen dramatically.

Sheriff Berkson watched as his officers picked up the orange cones and put them in the trunks of their cars. The road had been cleared of the smashed vehicles, and broken window glass had been removed from the highway. Lucky people, the Sheriff thought. No one died today.

Seeing that everything was under control, Sheriff Berkson got into his squad car and drove back towards the police station. He had just passed the Hollister city limits sign when his radio picked up a 911 call out on Trumpet Court. He hit his siren, turned off Hwy. 65 onto County Road BB, and headed up the hilly road.

The back of Charlie Hoppe's house was gone. The explosion had blown out a wall in his kitchen. Charlie, who had been walking from the living room into the kitchen, had been propelled back towards the front of his house, and out a picture window. He was lying in the front yard, covered with blood. He looked up as he saw the fire truck pull into his driveway. When he lifted his arm to indicate where he was, he realized his hand was missing.

As a fireman came running towards him, Charlie screamed, "My hand! It's in the house! Go find my fucking hand," and passed out.

Sheriff Berkson pulled into Charlie's driveway, got out of his car, and looked around. He watched as some of the firemen put out the scattered fires on the grass and the rest hosed down the inside of Charlie's house.

Fire Chief Whitman walked over to where Berkson was standing. "That was one hell of a big bang," he said to the Sheriff.

"Know what caused it?" Berkson asked.

"Not yet. We will, though, as soon as everything cools down. If I didn't know better, I'd say a bomb went off."

"Don't rule it out yet," Berkson told him.

"Do you know something I don't?" Whitman asked him.

"There seems to be a war going on around here. I'm pretty sure Cal Cuddihey is after Bobby. Charlie works for Bobby and it seems Charlie's most recent assignment has been to protect Bobby from someone –

160

probably Cal. Now, it looks like someone tried to blow Charlie up. Just might be that Cal is trying to get rid of Bobby's help."

"Reaching a little, aren't you, Sheriff?" Whitman asked.

"Probably. Let me know what you find out, will you?"

"It'll probably be a day or two before I'm done with my investigation."

"I can wait," said Berkson. "I'm goin' back to the office. Call me when you know something."

Fire Chief Whitman watched as the Sheriff got in his squad car and drove away, wondering if the Sheriff might be onto something or if it was just his imagination working overtime.

"So much for peace and quiet," Casey said. "How bad was it?"

"House is pretty much totaled," Sheriff Berkson told him. "Good thing Charlie is left-handed, 'cause his right hand was blown off."

"Does that mean that from now on he'll be one-handed? I wonder if he can do one-handed pushups. Gives a whole new meaning to 'can you lend me a hand', doesn't it?" Casey said, laughing.

161

Sheriff Berkson tried to hold back a grin. "That's not funny, Casey," he said.

"It kinda is. Do ya know why the one-handed man crossed the road?"

"That's enough, Casey," the Sheriff said.

"To get to the second-hand shop," Casey said, laughing.

Sheriff Berkson tried to hold back a laugh but didn't quite succeed.

"Sorry," Casey said. "So, what caused it? A gas leak?"

"Don't know yet, but I'm bettin' some type of explosive caused it."

"An explosive? Whataya mean? Like a bomb?"

"Exactly," replied the Sheriff.

Casey sat back in his chair and gazed at the Sheriff in surprise. "You think Cal Cuddihey did this, don't you?"

"Too soon to tell."

"Son of a bitch! You actually think that Cuddihey tried to kill Charlie, don't you?"

"It's a thought. We'll know for sure in a day or two. Until then, let's not jump to any conclusions."

Casey stood up and walked over to the coffee pot. "You know what, Cowboy?"

162

"What's that, Casey," the Sheriff asked.

"Peace and quiet is good. I mean it's nice when there's nobody doin' bad stuff. But I have to admit I like it when we got shit like this goin' on. Keeps us on the edge. Makes us use our brains to figure stuff out. Sometimes I get a real rush doing this job."

Sheriff Berkson smiled. "I know what you mean. Which is why I'm heading over to the hospital to see how Charlie is doing. It might be a good idea if I'm there when he gets out of surgery. You want to ride along?"

"Hell, yes. Let's go," Casey said and put the coffee pot back on the burner.

Bobby Johnson ended his phone call, reached over for his pain pills, and popped one into his mouth. Damn fool Charlie couldn't let it go, Bobby thought. "Karen," he yelled. "I need you."

Karen Berger, the newest nurse taking care of Bobby, ran into his room. "You okay, Bobby?" she asked.

"I'm fine. Will you stick your head out the door and tell Sammy to get in here?"

As Bobby waited impatiently for Sammy to come into his room, he swung his leg over the side of the bed, grabbed his crutches, and tried to stand.

"Wait, I'll help you," Sammy said, as he entered the room.

"I've got it. I just got a call. Charlie is in the hospital. He's in surgery right now. I want you to get over there. You need to be with him when he wakes up. Make sure he doesn't say anything stupid."

"What happened?" Sammy asked. "He told me he was goin' home for a little while to get some chores done."

"It seems his house blew up. He's in bad shape. I was told he lost one of his hands."

"Did Cal Cuddihey do it? It wouldn't surprise me one bit if that was the work of that bastard," Sammy said.

Bobby didn't say anything, thinking about how to answer. The last thing Bobby wanted was for Charlie to tell the authorities that he was messing around with explosives. He glanced over at Sammy, who was waiting for his answer. "You might be right. That just might be what happened. It might have been Cal's doing. When you get to the hospital, don't let the Sheriff or anyone question Charlie without you being there. You tell Charlie to play dumb and stay quiet. Got it?"

Sammy shook his head yes. "I got it, Bobby. I'll make sure that Charlie has no idea how it happened. I'll be sure all he remembers is a big bang and – what? What happened after that?"

"Tell him that all he remembers is an explosion and suddenly being on the ground in his front yard. That's all. That should be easy enough for him to remember. Maybe, he remembers seeing Cal driving around in that area before the explosion, too."

"Which hand did he lose?" Sammy asked.

"The right one."

"He's left-handed. He'll still be able to do a lot of stuff with just one hand."

"I don't think I'd mention that to him just now," Bobby replied.

Chapter Twenty-three

"Sorry, Sheriff, but I'm putting my foot down. He's in intensive care and no one's going in."

"I need to ask him a couple of questions. I'll be in and out of his room in seconds."

"Absolutely not," Dr. Wasserstein said. "I've seen how you question patients. You're not talking to Charlie until he's stable."

"How bad is it?"

"Whataya think? He was blown up. It's bad. He lost a lot of blood. I'm not sure if he's even going to make it."

"If that's the case, I really need to talk to him."

"Sheriff, listen to me. When Charlie's hand was blown off, the artery was severed. He lost about a third of his blood before the paramedics got there. Maybe, more. He sustained a head injury, which could be permanent. Plus, he has multiple cuts and injuries over his entire body. When I say he's in bad shape, I mean it. You are not – I repeat – you are not going in to see him."

Sheriff Berkson took a couple of steps back. He'd known Dr. Wasserstein for years, and could not remember him being as forceful as he was right now.

"Right. I got it, Doc. You want me to wait until he's feeling better before I talk to him."

"A lot better. I'll keep you informed, but there's no way you'll be seeing him for a while. I anticipate he'll be in intensive care for at least a week."

"That long, huh?" Sheriff Berkson asked.

"That long. Or, more."

"You'll keep me informed about his condition?" the Sheriff inquired.

"Of course. Now get out of here. I've got work to do."

Sammy Severson was sitting in the waiting room, his nose in a magazine, listening to Dr. Wasserstein and the Sheriff. He waited until the Sheriff and his deputy left the room, then he followed the doctor. "Excuse me," he called out.

Dr. Wasserstein turned and looked at him. "Something I can do for you?" he asked.

"Sorry to bother you, but Charlie Hoppe's a friend of mine. I was just wondering if you could give me an update on his condition."

Dr. Wasserstein sighed and shook his head from side to side. "Not unless you're family," he told him.

"Might as well be. Charlie and me are like brothers. I'm really worried about him, Doc. Can you tell me anything?"

167

"All I can say is that if you're a praying man, you should start praying. It doesn't look good."

"Are you saying he isn't gonna make it?" Sammy asked.

"It's in God's hands. I've done what I can."

Sheriff Berkson and Casey left the hospital and headed back towards the police station. Berkson was quiet, thinking about his conversation with the doctor. Suddenly, he turned off the highway and headed east.

"Where we going?" Casey asked.

"To Bobby Johnson's"

"What for?"

"It's time for him to start talking."

Casey didn't say anything for the rest of the ride, leaving the Sheriff to his thoughts. When they pulled up to Bobby's house, Casey finally spoke. "Whataya gonna ask him?"

"You see anyone patrolling?" the Sheriff asked.

Casey looked around. "Not in front. Might be somebody out back," Casey said.

"Wasn't that Sammy Severson at the hospital?" the Sheriff asked Casey.

"Where?"

"In the waiting room. It didn't hit me until now,

but I'm pretty sure he was there."

"I didn't notice him. If it was him, he was probably just waiting to see how Charlie's doing," Casey replied.

"Right. Okay, let's go in," the Sheriff said and got out of his car.

While waiting for someone to answer the door, Sheriff Berkson and Casey glanced around the yard but didn't see any activity. When no one answered the door, Casey hit the doorbell the second time. After a few more seconds, the door opened.

"May I help you," a good-looking woman inquired.

"Need to talk to Bobby," the Sheriff told her.

"He's sleeping."

"Then, wake him up."

"I can't do that. If you want to leave a message, I'll be sure he gets it."

"If you don't mind, I'd like to come in," the Sheriff said.

"I do mind. Now, if you'll excuse me, I've got work to do."

The woman shut the door, leaving Berkson and his deputy standing on the small porch.

The two men looked at each other, not quite sure what to make of what had just transpired.

"You want me to try again?" Casey asked the

Sheriff.

"Nah. Let's go." The Sheriff had a puzzled look on his face, as if trying to remember something. "Did she look familiar to you, Casey?"

Casey stood by the squad car, thinking about the Sheriff's question. "Sylvia Topper's sister," he finally exclaimed. "What was her name? Alice – no. Wait – I've got it. Olivia. That's it. That was Olivia. From Texas."

Sheriff Berkson got in the car and started it up. "Wonder what the hell she's doing here?" he said.

"And, what work could she possibly be doing for Bobby?" commented Casey.

"Who was it?" Bobby asked.

"That Sheriff and his shadow."

"Casey?" Bobby asked.

"Right."

"Did he say what he wanted?"

"Just that he wanted to talk to you. I told him you were sleeping."

"Thanks. I'm not in the mood to deal with him."

"I figured. Should we pick up where we were before the doorbell rang?"

"Where'd you say Karen was?" Bobby asked.

"I sent her to get some groceries. A long list of

groceries. She won't be back for a while."

"Then, let's go for it," Bobby said and smiled as Olivia dove headfirst under his covers.

A few days earlier, Bobby had talked to Olivia and asked if she'd like to come up and visit for a few days. He told her that he'd send his plane down to Corpus Christi and fly her back to Branson. Olivia, who was ready to get away for a few days, told her ex to watch the kids and was waiting at the airport when Bobby's plane arrived to pick her up.

Bobby had been having an on-again-off-again affair with her since he had flown to Corpus Christi for her sister's funeral. Olivia was a couple of years older than Sylvia, but they could have passed for twins. Bobby cared a lot for Olivia, but he had loved Sylvia, who had been murdered.

He knew Olivia wasn't interested in making the move to Hollister. He had suggested she pack up and move into Sylvia's house, but she said no. Her children's father and her job were down in Texas, and she wanted to remain there. So, Bobby flew her in every so often, they would enjoy each other's company for a few days, and she'd fly back home.

Olivia was the one person that he could talk to

about his brothers. Although he never told her the whole story about his mother's death, he told her about Sylvia's part in framing Big John for her murder. He concocted a story of how someone had smothered his mother and how he had used the opportunity to set up his two brothers, so he could inherit his mother's entire estate. Olivia had kept quiet for several reasons. One - she was really fond of Bobby. Two - she didn't want to damage her sister's reputation. And, three - she was the sole beneficiary of Sylvia's estate, of which the majority was the payoff from Bobby for testifying against Big John. She had no intentions of losing that money, so she kept Bobby's secrets.

This time, however, besides sex, Bobby had an ulterior motive for asking Olivia to spend a few days with him. He had explained to her what had been going on since the boat accident, that he needed a hitman and why. She agreed to check around Corpus Christi and see if there was someone in her area who was up for the job.

Olivia had only been at Bobby's for about an hour when they had been interrupted by the doorbell. Get rid of whoever it is and get your beautiful ass back in this bed, Bobby had told her. And, Olivia had done exactly that.

Chapter Twenty-four

Officer Funtelli was sitting in his squad car, which was parked on Harper Lane. He had been observing Bobby Johnson's house for days. He wanted to know the routine of the people working for Bobby, but so far, he couldn't get a handle on it. There didn't seem to be a set pattern for anyone. Since Charlie's accident, Sammy Severson was spending some nights with Bobby. Sometimes, however, he went home for the night and, on one occasion, his wife had stayed with him at Bobby's. It was almost impossible to determine what nurse was working when, or if there was even more than one working. John Luke and some other guy he didn't recognize hung around the yard, carrying their guns and pacing back and forth. They'd stop and talk a while and then continue their surveillance.

Doc Messerly had shown up once, spent about twenty minutes in the house, and left. Recently, while Funtelli was watching the house, he saw a woman come out carrying a small overnight bag. John Luke pulled one of Bobby's cars up to the front door, she got in, and he drove her away. Funtelli thought she looked familiar, but he couldn't place her.

Funtelli jumped when his radio broke the silence. He hesitated before he pushed the button. "Hey, Brad.

What's up?"

"Sheriff wants you back at the station. Stat!"

"Is there a problem?"

"I don't think so. He just told me to tell you to get back here now."

"On my way," Funtelli responded.

"Where are you, anyway?" Officer Brad Herzberg asked him.

"Near Ken's Gas Station. I'll be there in a few."

"10-4," Brad said and cut off the communication.

"He's gone," Sammy told Bobby.

"How long was he here this time?" Bobby asked him.

"About an hour. Maybe a little more. What do you think he's doing out there?"

"Obviously, he's watching the house," Bobby answered.

"What for?"

"What? I'm a mind reader now? How the hell should I know what for?"

"You think the Sheriff sent him?" Sammy asked.

"Probably. I called and reported it. If the Sheriff didn't know about it, he does now."

"I saw Cuddihey's truck drive by," Sammy

174

commented.

Bobby's head jerked up. He stared at Sammy. "When? When was that?"

"Early this morning. He drove by real slow, staring at the house."

"Tell John Luke and Phil to be on their toes. I wouldn't put it past Cal to try something again."

"I'm on it. You need anything?"

"Ya. Tell Karen I could use a back rub."

"Where the hell you been, Funtelli? I hardly see you anymore."

"Just out patrolling," Funtelli answered.

"You could check in once in a while."

"Sorry."

"You writing a lot of tickets?" the Sheriff asked.

"Not really. I don't know what's goin' on. It's like everybody just got their driver's license and they're afraid they'll get a ticket on the first day that they're legal."

"So, no tickets?"

"Not so far today."

The Sheriff stared at Funtelli for a few seconds. "Not a lot of traffic up there on Harper Lane?" he said sarcastically.

Funtelli looked surprised but didn't answer the Sheriff.

"How about near Ken's Gas Station? Didn't you find anyone speeding there either?"

Funtelli looked away.

"Bobby Johnson called in a complaint, Simon," the Sheriff said quietly. "He complained that you've been watching his house. Said he's feeling harassed. Are you sitting in your car spying on him, while you should be working?"

Funtelli smiled. "It's not like that," he said. "I was up there, okay? But, not spying on him. More like - you know - protecting him. With what happened to Charlie, and Bobby's house being shot up . . . Well, I thought I'd drive by a few times a day. You know. . ."

Funtelli quit talking when he saw the look on the Sheriff's face.

"Quit the bullshit, Simon. Just who the hell do you think you're talking to?" the Sheriff yelled. "I don't know what you're up to, but it stops now. Got it?"

"I'm not up to anything," Funtelli muttered.

"And, if I find out this has anything to do with JoJo, I'll suspend you for a month."

"Are you done?"

Sheriff Berkson sat back in his chair, mouth open,

glaring at Funtelli. "What did you say?"

"Nothing."

"Get out of here, Simon, before I do something I'll regret. I don't want to see your ugly face for the rest of the day."

Funtelli stared back at the Sheriff, broke eye contact, turned, and walked out of the police station.

Deputy George let out a deep breath. "He needs help, Sheriff. His whole personality has changed since JoJo showed up. His fuse is lit and he's gonna explode any minute."

"I think you might be right. I handled that all wrong just now. Getting him angrier isn't gonna help matters."

"Whataya gonna do?" Casey asked.

"I'll give him a while to cool down. Then, I'll talk to him."

"Hey, Sheriff," Officer Herzberg hollered. "Call for you. It's the Fire Chief, Bob Whitman."

The Sheriff picked up the phone. "Whatcha find out?" he said.

"Hello, to you, too, Cowboy," Whitman replied.

"Sorry."

"It was definitely a bomb," Whitman told the Sheriff.

"You sure?"

"We found pieces of it scattered around the house. No question in my mind. Someone tried to kill Charlie Hoppe. You've got a murder on your hands, Sheriff."

"Anything else that might give us a clue as to who did this?"

"Sorry. I can't help you there. Have you heard how Charlie is doing?"

"He's still in intensive care. He's hanging in there. His doctor still won't let me talk to him, though."

"He'll be lucky if he makes it. You may never get any answers from him."

"Let's hope that doesn't happen."

"You still think it was Cuddihey's doing?" Whitman asked.

"I'd bet my bottom dollar on it," replied the Sheriff.

"Well, good luck with that. I'll let you know if I find anything else."

"Thanks, Chief."

Chapter Twenty-five

Sammy stopped by the hospital on the chance he could get some information regarding his friend. He knew that the staff was more likely to tell him face to face how Charlie was feeling, than on the phone. When he went to the nurses' station in the ICU, he talked to a sweet young nurse, who told him that Charlie was awake. He asked if he could talk to him for a minute, and she told him that would be fine. Not too long, though, she had added.

Sammy hesitated as he walked into Charlie's room. Charlie looked a lot worse than he anticipated.

"It's that bad, huh," Charlie asked him, seeing the alarmed look on his friend's face.

"Have you looked in a mirror?" Sammy asked.

"Haven't had the chance."

"Don't. You'll break it for sure," Sammy said.

"That woulda happened even before I was blown up," Charlie replied, snickering.

"What the hell happened?" Sammy asked.

"I thought I could make a bomb, so I could blow up Cuddihey. I wanted to take care of Bobby's problem, plus I figured I could put some extra cash to good use. Bobby told me to forget it, but I figured I'd try it anyway. Damn thing just went off. I don't know what I did wrong,

179

but my bomb-making days are over for sure."

"You think?" Sammy said. "You're lucky to be alive, Charlie.

"I guess, but having one hand is gonna be a real pain in the ass. I'll probably get one of those prosathatics."

"You mean prosthetics," Sammy said, correcting him.

"Right. I've been thinking about a new nickname for myself. Got any ideas?"

Sammy laughed. "I'm glad you're taking this so well. Has anyone from the police department been here to talk to you?"

"Not yet. Why?"

Sammy spent the next few minutes prepping Charlie as to what Bobby wanted him to say when the police interviewed him. As he listened to the plan, Charlie shook his head in agreement.

"You got it, then?" Sammy asked.

Charlie gave him a left thumbs up. If the Sheriff believed Charlie's story, Cal Cuddihey was in trouble.

An ICU nurse stuck her head in Charlie's room and smiled at the two men. "Sorry, but I'm gonna have to ask you to leave now. Charlie needs to get some rest."

Timing sure is everything, Sammy thought, as he drove out of the hospital's parking lot onto the street. A Hollister squad car, driven by Sheriff Berkson, was just pulling into a parking spot.

"I'm sorry, Sheriff, but he needs his rest. I'm not going to wake Mr. Hoppe so you can talk to him."

"Is Dr. Wasserstein here?" Sheriff Berkson asked the nurse.

"Not at the moment. However, Dr. Wasserstein made it clear to us that you are not allowed in Mr. Hoppe's room without his permission."

"He said that?"

"He did. Mr. Hoppe is very weak and the doctor doesn't want him to get agitated. Besides, he's already had one visitor this morning."

Berkson looked surprised. "And, who would that be?"

"I don't know the man's name. He said he's a relative of Mr. Hoppe."

"Where's the doc?" Berkson asked. "I want to talk to him now."

"I don't keep track of the doctors. I'm sorry. I suggest you give him a call. Other than that, there's nothing else I can do."

Sheriff Berkson watched as the nurse turned and walked away. He walked out of the ICU area into a waiting room. He took out his phone and called the station.

"Brad," he said. "see if you can find out where Doctor Wasserstein is. I'm at the hospital and I want to talk to him."

"Did you talk to Charlie?" Brad asked him.

"The staff has instructions not to let me in to see him. I need to find out what's going on with the doc. I'll wait here until I hear back from you."

"My god, Bobby. You should see him. I don't know how he survived that blast. He's a total mess. Just the parts of him that I could see are covered with bandages. His neck and face are gonna be scarred so bad. He's a better man than I am. If that was me in that hospital, I'd be hating the world and everyone in it. He's even excited about getting a prosthetic hand. I figured he'd be depressed about this, but he's joking about getting a new nickname."

"You told him the plan? About telling the Sheriff that he saw Cal driving around in his area before the explosion? You told him everything we talked about?"

"Yep. He knows what to say. You wanna know the

182

best part?"

"What's that?"

It's fate. I decide to stop in to see him this morning and I get to talk to him. Then, as I'm leaving, the Sheriff is pulling into the parking lot? I'll bet anything he was there to see Charlie. If I'd showed up fifteen minutes later, the Sheriff would have talked to him already."

"So, you think the Sheriff is with him now?"

"I'd bet my boots on it."

"Well, it was either fate or just good timing. Thanks, Sammy."

"How's your leg feeling today, Bobby? I never hear you complain about it."

"Pills help. It's getting better. I'll be glad when the cast is off for good and I can start walking on it."

"It's not even three weeks yet."

"I know. Just saying. I'm thinking about getting out of here for a while. Maybe, take a ride and get some fresh air.

"Do you think that's wise? You know, with what's going on?"

Bobby shrugged. "I feel like a prisoner in my own home. Wise or not – I'm going for a ride this afternoon."

"You got any orange juice?" Sammy asked.

"Probably."

"You want something to drink," Sammy asked as he walked towards the kitchen.

"Ya, bring me a glass of juice. I gotta hand it to Charlie. He's a tough guy. I'm glad he's on my side. So, Charlie wants a new nickname, does he? Did you come up with any?" Bobby asked.

"Not really. I think a nickname just happens. Can't be something you pick for yourself. If this happened years ago, they'd just fit him with a hook and he'd probably be called that. Hook, I mean. Medicine sure has come a long way. Some of those fake limbs look real."

Bobby's face lit up. "That's it!" he exclaimed. "Sammy you're a genius."

Sammy looked confused. "What? What did I say?"

Bobby was grinning. "There's a shoebox on the shelf in my closet. Go get it for me, will ya?"

"What's going on, Bobby?"

"I gotta make a phone call."

"You want me to get your phone, too?"

"No. Just get the box."

"You don't want your phone?"

"No."

"How you gonna make a call without your phone?"

184

"With a burner phone. I keep a few handy, just in case I need one. Like now."

Sheriff Berkson was standing in the waiting room of the hospital, looking out the window and watching the traffic on Branson Landing Blvd. He jumped when he felt a tap on his shoulder.

"Didn't mean to scare you there, Cowboy," Doctor Wasserstein said, laughing.

"Just in another world, Doc," the Sheriff replied, as he turned and faced the doctor.

"I hear you need to speak to me."

"I do, Doc. I'd like to know why you won't let me talk to Charlie Hoppe. What's the deal?"

"I told you that it might be a week before you could question him."

"That might be what you said, but he had a visitor this morning. So, why can't I see him?" the Sheriff asked.

"I didn't approve visitors. Do you know who it was?"

"No. But, if he's well enough to talk to whoever it was, then I should be able to ask him a few questions," the Sheriff said, emphatically.

"I haven't finished my rounds yet this morning. I'll

check on Charlie and see how he's doing. I think you can probably talk to him, but let's wait until this afternoon. How about I meet you around three o'clock?"

"Why can't I go talk to him now? I'm here. No sense in coming back."

"I just said I need to finish my rounds."

Berkson looked confused. "Why can't I go without you?"

"You're serious, aren't you?"

"Of course, I am,"

"Well, Sheriff, it's been decided here at the hospital that any time you need to talk to a suspect, an accident victim, or anyone that isn't family or a friend, someone from the staff needs to be with you."

The Sheriff's mouth dropped open in surprise. "I don't get it," he said.

"Just think Walter White. We can't have that kind of stuff going on here again. You practically tortured that man."

"Well, he confessed, didn't he?"

"Sorry, Sheriff. Them's the rules. From now on, you need to be accompanied by a staff member when you question someone."

Chapter Twenty-six

Hook wanted to buy a boat.

It only took one phone call from Bobby to convince Steve "Hook" Salitore to do the job. A few years ago, Bobby had paid him a hefty sum for his help in framing his brother, Tom. At the time, Hook figured that the money he received would allow him to live comfortably on the islands for the rest of his life. He also knew that if he spent any of it on a boat, he'd be broke. He really wanted a boat. So, when Bobby made him an offer to do another job for him, Hook jumped on it.

Bobby told Hook he would immediately wire half the money into an offshore account and the rest when the job was done. Hook confirmed that his fake passport was still good, so getting in and out of the States shouldn't be a problem.

"Let me handle it," Hook had said. "You don't need to know the details."

"You're sure about this?" Bobby had asked. "I know we agreed that you would never set foot in Missouri again. Or, any of the States, for that matter. You'll be taking a big risk coming back here to do this. And, this has to be the last time, Hook. You can never come back here again.

"Noted, my friend. And, I'm as sure about this as I

am that the sun will shine here tomorrow. You're living in the wrong part of the world, Bobby. You should move here. This is paradise personified. I wouldn't even think about leaving here and risk coming back to the States, except I want to buy a boat."

Bobby had laughed. "Must be one hell of a big boat."

"She's more beautiful than big. I'm in love with her."

"I guess we'll both get what we want, then. Thanks, Hook. By the way, don't call this number. It's a burner phone and I'm dumping it. Call Sammy Severson if you need to get a message to me. But, only in case of an emergency. Otherwise, I don't want to talk to you again. Got it?"

"Got it. Take care, Bobby." And, before Bobby could reply, the phone went dead.

"Pick up Cal Cuddihey. He's got some explaining to do," Sheriff Berkson said, as he walked into the police station.

"Now?" Casey asked.

"Of course, now."

Casey looked puzzled. "Where does he work? I know where he lives, but I don't know where he works."

Sheriff Berkson looked at Casey and shrugged his shoulders. "Hell, if I know. I thought you knew."

"I don't know. Does he even have a job?"

"Of course, he does. At least I think he does."

Casey sat at his desk, thinking. "I guess I can drive out to his house and see if he's there."

"I heard Katie's parents are taking care of the kids now – they're living with them. If you don't find Cal at home, drive over and ask Katie's parents where he works."

"Or, I could just call them," Casey commented, as he got up from his desk and left.

Cal Cuddihey was as mad as a corralled bull at a Santa Claus convention. He was, in fact, being restrained at this very moment. Cuddihey was in handcuffs, being dragged into the police station by Deputy George, and Officers Carlson and Herzberg.

Casey shoved him into an interrogation room and told him to sit down before he tased the crap out of him. Cuddihey plunked his ass in the chair and yelled. "Take these damn cuffs off me. They're too tight." Casey gave him a disgusted look and left the room.

Sheriff Berkson looked Casey up and down. "I guess you shoulda took some help with you when you left."

"You think?" Casey said. "That man's crazy, Sheriff. I swear he would have killed me if I hadn't pulled my gun."

"What the hell did you say to him that made him go off on you? By, the way, you better get some ice on that eye. It's already turning color."

"All I said was that you wanted to talk to him. I asked if he wanted to follow me or I could give him a ride. He wanted to know what for, and when I told him I didn't know for sure, he refused. Then, I said that he either comes with me voluntarily or I'd have to cuff him."

"Then he hit you?"

"He did. Punched me in the face and told me to get the hell off his property. Damn, this wouldn't have happened if Funtelli was with me."

"Then what?" the Sheriff asked.

"I got up, went to the car, and requested backup. Carlson and Herzberg showed up, we subdued him, and brought him in."

"He only hit you once?"

"Once was enough."

"All right. I'll talk to him. Go get some ice on that eye."

Sheriff Berkson waited for a half-hour before he walked into the room where Cuddihey was waiting. He pulled out a chair, sat down, and looked at Cal.

"What's wrong with you, Cal?" he asked. "You just hit one of my officers. You know you could go to jail for that, don't you?"

"He pissed me off. He's got a real smart mouth, you know. I didn't need his crap – wasn't in the mood for it - and I asked him to leave. Then, he got all tough acting and tried to cuff me. So, I hit him. Nobody cuffs me, Sheriff. Nobody."

"Well, Cal, it looks to me like you're cuffed right now."

"Ya, but it took three of them to do it."

"I just wanted to talk to you. Just ask you a few questions. Now, I've got to arrest you. You've made it tougher on yourself."

"Whataya wanna talk to me for?" Cuddihey asked.

"You were seen hanging around Charlie Hoppe's house before it blew up. What were you doing out there, Cal?"

"Whoever said that is lying. I haven't been near Charlie's house."

"The way I figure it, you're trying to get at Bobby and the only way you'll be able to do that is to get rid of

191

his security people."

Cal gave a nasty laugh. "Security people. Is that what you're calling them? Why, they're nothing more than a couple of red necks spending the day walking around that big ass trailer of Bobby's, carrying guns and acting tough."

"Mobile home," the Sheriff corrected.

"What?"

"It's not a trailer. It's a mobile home."

"So, who gives a fuck what you call it?"

Sheriff Berkson smiled a little, as his mind flashed back to a few years ago. Melissa did, he thought. Man, she would get so mad when you called her home a trailer. Another good life wasted, and for what? It's a crazy world . . .

"Sheriff?" Cal said, wondering if Berkson was okay.

"Why are you trying to kill Bobby Johnson?"

"What?" Cuddihey asked, surprised at the bluntness of the question. He hesitated a second and said, "I'm not. Bobby's a friend of mine. Why would I want to kill him?"

"That's what I just asked you. You know what I think. I think you tried to shoot Bobby, missed him and the bullet hit his nurse. I think that when you ran that boat into the dock, you were trying to kill yourself, your wife, and Bobby. It was no accident and I know it. You killed Katie who, in my opinion, is the only one who should have lived. This world can do without dirt like you and Bobby Johnson, but she was a good lady."

Cal Cuddihey was fuming, his face turning red, as he listened to the Sheriff.

"She was a fucking whore!" he screamed. "You don't know anything. You think I killed her? Then, fucking prove it. You think I shot at Bobby? Prove it! You have nothing." He glared at the Sheriff. "And, as far as Charlie Hoppe is concerned – well, I wouldn't give him the time of day. You got that all wrong, too." He glared at the Sheriff in disgust. "I don't know how you keep your job."

The Sheriff didn't react to Cal's ranting. He waited until Cal sat back in his chair, giving him time to cool off. After a few minutes, he got up and left the room.

"Get me some water, will ya, Brad?" he asked.

"How's it going in there?" Brad asked.

"He really does have one bad temper. I doubt we'll get anything out of him, but you never know. Sometimes, a slip of the tongue is all you need to close a case."

"You think he's telling the truth?"

"Nah. He's lying through his teeth. At least, about the boat accident and trying to shoot Bobby." The Sheriff shrugged. "I'm not sure about the bomb thing with Charlie, though. I kinda think he didn't do that."

"You gonna let him go?"

"He hit Casey. Gotta arrest him. He'll probably make bail tomorrow, though," the Sheriff replied.

"Too bad it isn't Friday. He'd have to sit in county for the weekend."

"Right. Well, back to work," Sheriff Berkson said and walked back into the interrogation room.

Chapter Twenty-seven

Around 12:30 a.m. Sunday night, Cal Cuddihey stumbled out of Waxy's Bar and headed in the direction where he thought he had parked his car. After starting an argument with the couple sitting next to him, the bartender had told him to leave. He had gone quietly, just sober enough to realize he could wind up back in jail if the bartender decided to call the cops.

On Friday, it had taken nearly all of his savings to pay the bond to get out of jail. He had hit a cop and there was a possibility that he could wind up in prison. His attorney had told him that the least he would get is probation and probably a stiff fine.

Cal couldn't stop being angry. He was angry because Bobby Johnson was still living and his own life had been destroyed. He'd lost everything. His wife, his kids, and his best friend. His job was in jeopardy, and he was drinking way too much. All because of that damned Bobby Johnson.

He tripped and almost fell to the ground as he staggered towards his car. He grabbed the side mirror of a car next to him and steadied himself. He stood there for a couple of seconds trying to remember where he had parked his car. He took one more step before a bullet struck him between his eyes. Dead, he fell backwards against a car that was parked behind him, and slowly slid to the ground.

A lone figure walked to where Cuddihey was lying, looked down at the body, and smiled. He felt around on the ground, looking for Cuddihey's car keys. He found them next to Cuddihey's right hand and picked them up. Then, he walked a few feet to Cuddihey's car and unlocked the trunk. He reached into his pocket, pulled out a couple of items, and tossed them into the trunk. He walked back to where Cuddihey's body was lying and laid the keys next to his body. He wasn't concerned about leaving fingerprints, as he was wearing gloves. He glanced around, felt secure that no one had seen him, and walked away.

Cal's body was found an hour later by the same couple that had been sitting next to him in the bar. They called 911, went back into the bar for another drink, and waited for the cops to arrive.

Officer Zeke Bell, working the night shift, had gotten the call about a body being found at Waxy's Bar. With sirens blaring and lights flashing, he made it to the bar in record time. When he identified the body as Cal Cuddihey, he immediately called the Sheriff, waking him up. Sheriff Berkson told him to secure the scene, not touch anything, and wait for him to get there.

Sheriff Berkson pulled into Waxy's parking lot and got out of his squad car. He looked around and determined that all of Hollister's patrol cars were there. Good, he thought. We're gonna need all the help we can get tonight.

Berkson walked under the orange tape that had been strung to cordon off the crime scene and waved at Officer Bell. Bell walked over to him, shaking his head. "It's Cal Cuddihey, Sheriff. From what I can tell, one shot right between the eyes. I didn't touch the body, so there could be more. We'll know more when the coroner gets here."

"Have you called Doc Harris?"

"He's on his way," Officer Bell replied.

"Who found him," the Sheriff asked.

"A couple walking to their car. They're the ones who called it in. They're in the bar waiting to talk to you."

"Who else did you talk to?"

"The bartender. He said that Cuddihey was asked to leave the bar after getting loud and trying to start a fight with a couple of people. He told him to leave or he was gonna call 911. Cuddihey left around 12:30 a.m."

"What time was he found?" the Sheriff asked.

"About an hour or so later. The couple he was fighting with in the bar are the ones who found him."

Sheriff Berkson walked over to where Cuddihey was lying on the ground. He bent down, shined his flashlight on Cuddihey's face, and looked at the entry wound.

"No powder residue that I can see right now. Bag those car keys next to him there, Zeke. Find his car, too. We'll need to take a close look at that."

Zeke gloved up, bent down, and picked up the keys. He pushed a button on the remote and a car horn sounded. "That's his car, over there," he said to the Sheriff.

"I'm gonna go talk to that couple in the bar," Sheriff Berkson said. "Wait here for Doc Harris. Let me know when he gets here." He turned and walked towards the bar. He stopped and turned around. "Zeke, see if we can get more lights out here, will ya?"

At 5:00 a.m. the last cop car pulled out of Waxy's parking lot. Cal Cuddihey's body was at the morgue, awaiting an autopsy. His car had been towed to the station, so forensics could go through it. Sheriff Berkson

198

had gone home to take a shower, shave, and get some breakfast.

Now, two hours later, the Sheriff was sitting at his desk, going over the reports his officers had handed in. Not much to go on, he thought. The bartender stated that Cuddihey was argumentative and had been asked to leave around 12:30 a.m. The couple who found the body weren't considered suspects, as other customers in the bar verified that they were in the bar for at least an hour after Cuddihey had left. No one had heard a shot. That made sense, as there was loud music playing inside the bar, and that would have muffled outside noises.

Sheriff Berkson walked over to the coffee machine and poured another cup of coffee. He stretched his body to its full six feet, trying to get the kinks out. It had been a long night and it looked like it would be a long day. He sighed, sat back down at his desk, and continued going over the statements made by patrons of the bar.

Bobby Johnson wanted to dance. He was in the kitchen, going through the cupboards, looking for a bottle of Jack Daniels Tennessee Whiskey. It didn't make any difference that it was four o'clock in the morning. He wanted to celebrate. Cal Cuddihey was

199

dead. He could finally stop looking over his shoulder and relax.

"Sammy, get in here," he practically screamed.

A few seconds later, Sammy and his night nurse, Janice, came running into the kitchen.

Sammy stopped in his tracks when he saw Bobby standing by the table, leaning on his crutches.

"What the hell, Bobby? I thought you were being murdered."

"Where's the Jack?" Bobby asked, grinning ear to ear.

"The what?" Janice asked.

"Where the fuck is my whiskey? I want a drink."

"Bobby," Janice said, patronizingly, "you're on pain killers. You can't have alcohol."

"You know what, Janice baby? I can have any fucking thing I want. And, right now I want a nice stiff drink." He glanced over at Sammy and asked him, "Where's my booze? Did you guys drink it?"

"What's going on, Bobby," Sammy asked. "Why in the world do you need a drink at – what time is it? Four o'clock? It's four in the morning, for crying out loud."

Bobby smiled at Janice. "Leave us alone, will you? I need to talk to Sammy."

Janice shook her head in disgust and exited the

kitchen, muttering under her breath.

"Cuddihey is dead," Bobby whispered to Sammy.

"Are you serious? How do you know?"

"I just got a phone call. Cal was killed in Waxy's parking lot. A bullet to the head. He's dead, Sammy. Do you know what that means?"

"Ya. It means I'm out of a job."

"I need to sit," Bobby said. "Is there any booze left in this house?"

"It's in the pantry. Phil has a drinking problem, so we hid it in there."

"Well, get it, would ya?"

Sammy opened the door to the pantry, reached behind some cereal boxes, and pulled out a bottle of Jack Daniels. He poured a couple of stiff drinks and handed one to Bobby.

"Thanks," Bobby said. "Sit."

Sammy sat down and took a sip of his drink.

"You're not out of a job, Sammy. At least, not for a while. How about taking over Charlie's job?"

Sammy grinned. "That would be great, Bobby. Just what did Charlie do, anyway?"

"For starters, he was my driver when I didn't want to drive myself. He did odd jobs for me, washed my cars and trucks, ran errands, and did whatever I needed. It's

201

gonna be a long time before he'll be able to do anything. Whataya say? You want the job?"

"Hell, yes, I want the job."

"Done. The other thing - starting tomorrow I want the nurses gone. All they're doing is sitting around, reading, and watching TV. I can pretty much take care of myself. The physical therapist comes twice a week. I figure that's all I need for now."

"I'll take care of it. What about John Luke and Phil?"

"Don't need them anymore either. You can tell them tomorrow that they're through," Bobby replied.

"Do you still want me to spend the nights? I don't think you should be alone yet."

"Maybe, you should. At least, for a while. I've got a few weeks to go before I start walking on this leg. It might be a good idea if you stayed nights. Tell Alicia she's welcome to join you any time she feels like it." Bobby finished his drink and put the glass on the table. "Pour me one more, will ya. I doubt I'll be able to get back to sleep. Another drink might help."

"You got it, Boss," Sammy said, grinning.

Chapter Twenty-eight

As soon as the sun was up, the Sheriff sent Officers Carlson and Herzberg back to Waxy's Bar. He told them to comb the area where Cal Cuddihey had been murdered, hoping they might find some evidence that had been overlooked in the dark.

At the police station, Sheriff Berkson and some of his fellow policemen were looking at the items that had been removed from the trunk of Cuddihey's car.

"I can't believe it," Casey exclaimed. "How could he be so stupid as to leave this stuff in the trunk of his car?"

"I never figured he was real smart," said Officer Bell, "but this is way beyond stupid. He knew we suspected him of blowing up Charlie, so why didn't he get rid of this stuff?"

Sheriff Berkson shook his head. "You just never know what goes on in the heads of people," he remarked. "I'll bet you anything that this matches the stuff that was used to make that bomb. Cal might as well have left a note saying he did it."

"It's almost like he wanted to be caught," said Casey. "It's too bad we didn't find the gun that shot that nurse, too."

"Still might. We're not done searching his house

and outbuildings yet," the Sheriff pointed out.

"Sounds like Herzberg and Carlson are back," the Sheriff remarked when he heard a noise coming from the back of the police station.

"They've been gone a long time," Casey noted.

"Since sun up. Let's hope they found something we can use," the Sheriff responded.

"We found a casing," Officer Herzberg stated, as he walked into the room.

"Where'd you find it?"

"In the weeds. About fifteen feet back in from the parking lot. I took pictures before we bagged it."

"Find anything else?" the Sheriff asked.

"You don't wanna know. God, people are pigs," said Officer Carlson.

"It looks like the shooter was about 70 feet away when he pulled the trigger," Herzberg added.

"If that's right, that's a hell of a shot. What kind of a casing did you find?" the Sheriff asked.

"A 9mm," Herzberg replied.

"Cuddihey was killed by a 9mm. It's probably from the shooter's gun. Good work, guys."

Casey met the Sheriff's eyes.

"What?" the Sheriff asked.

"I was just wondering – you know – about Katie

Cuddihey's death. We've figured all along that Cal ran that boat into the dock on purpose. Now that Cal's gone, maybe Bobby will tell us what really happened. Do you think we should go talk to him?"

The Sheriff thought about Casey's question for a few seconds. "I think that's a good idea, Casey. If Bobby will tell us what happened, we can close that case, too. The only thing we'll probably never know, for sure, is who shot that nurse. And, we're all pretty sure – like 100% sure – that it was Cal who did that drive by. I'll go out and talk to Bobby first thing tomorrow."

It had been five days since Officer Funtelli had been chewed out by the Sheriff for lying about watching Bobby's house. Rather than stop spying on Bobby, Funtelli decided to just change his routine.

Each day since then, during the first few hours that he was on duty, he wrote as many tickets as he could. He showed no mercy, citing drivers for even the slightest violation. Then, he would drive up to Harper Lane and, for the next fifteen or twenty minutes, he would watch Bobby Johnson's house. He repeated this routine until his shift was over. He wrote more tickets during the five or six hours that he actually worked, than ever before.

On Monday, as he sat in his squad car and watched Bobby's house, Funtelli realized that something was different. It finally hit him that he hadn't seen any guards. No one was walking the perimeter. Interesting, he thought. Cuddihey is dead and Bobby calls off his dogs. He watched the house for a few more minutes and drove off.

As soon as his shift was over, Funtelli went home, changed clothes, and drove up the hill to Bobby's house. He watched the house long enough to determine, once more, that Bobby's house was no longer being guarded. Then, he pulled into Bobby's driveway, got out, and rang the bell.

"What the hell do you want, Funtelli?" Sammy asked as he opened the door.

"Can I talk to Bobby?"

Sammy turned away from Funtelli and yelled, "Hey, Bobby, Funtelli wants to talk to you. Are you home?"

"Sure am. Send him in."

Bobby was sitting in a recliner, in the living room, watching TV. He hit the remote and muted the sound. "What brings you out here, Funtelli?"

"Just wanted to see how you're doing, Bobby.

How's the leg?"

"Better each day. According to my doctor, I'll be walking on two legs pretty soon. Can't wait."

"Did you hear that Cal Cuddihey is dead?" Funtelli asked.

"I did. I was real sorry to hear that. He was a good friend of mine. Thank god those two little kids have their grandparents to take care of them."

"Amen, to that," Funtelli said, shaking his head in agreement.

"I'm Pat's godfather, you know," Bobby told him. "I'll be sure those kids won't want for anything. I'm setting up a college fund for them."

"That's really generous of you, Bobby."

"Least I can do," Bobby said, wiping a tear from his eye.

"It's really sad," Funtelli said. "By the way, how's Charlie doing?"

"He's doing good. At first, I thought we might lose him, but he's tough. He may be outta the hospital next week."

"Well, that's good news," Funtelli said.

"You want a drink?" Bobby suddenly asked.

"Na, I'm good. I just wanted to see how you're doing. I'll be on my way and let you get your rest."

"Well, thanks for stopping by. I appreciate it."

"You still got those good-looking nurses working for you?" Funtelli asked, as he stood up to leave.

"Nope. Don't need them anymore. Now, I just see the physical therapist a few times a week."

"I hear water therapy works great. That big old pool of yours should help with that. Man, that's a great pool."

"Any time you want to take a swim, stop by."

Funtelli took a few steps closer to Bobby, reached out, and shook his hand. "Thanks. I just might do that. See you around, Bobby."

"See you, Funtelli," Bobby answered and watched Funtelli as he closed the door.

"What the hell was that all about?" Sammy asked.

Bobby gave him a blank look. "I have no fucking idea."

Chapter Twenty-nine

"Who fixed the outside of your house?" Casey asked.

"What?"

"You can't see the bullet hole. Who did the work?"

"Falconi's Home Repair. They did a nice job, didn't they?' Bobby replied.

"You been outside?" Sheriff Berkson asked.

"Once or twice. It's hard to maneuver the stairs, but I'm getting the hang of it."

"Can you drive?" Casey asked.

"Are you kidding? Driving again is way in the future. Gotta learn how to walk first without these damned crutches."

"Were you home Sunday night?" the Sheriff inquired.

Bobby looked the Sheriff in the eye. "That's probably one of the more stupid questions you've ever asked. Of course, I was here. I've been here every day since I left the hospital. And, before you even bother to ask me – no, I did not shoot Cal."

"Who was with you Sunday night or were you alone?" the Sheriff asked.

"Who was here? Let me think. Janice Hallman was working the night shift. Sammy was here. He stayed the whole night. John Luke and Phil Wilson were patrolling outside. I guess that's it."

"So, you can alibi each other. Convenient."

"Not convenient. True. Sheriff, none of us shot Cal, if that's what you're getting at," Bobby stated.

"Okay. Then, I wonder if you'd give me your version of what happened the day Cal crashed your boat?"

"I already have."

"Humor me. Tell me again," the Sheriff said.

"I'm telling you, Sheriff, it was an accident," Bobby exclaimed, emphatically.

"That's not what I'm hearing, Bobby. Rumor is you were messing around with Katie and Cal found out. Why not just fess up? Cal's dead. You don't have anything to worry about now."

"Well, the rumor is wrong. Cal and I were friends."

"He tried to shoot you. Since when do friends do that to each other?"

"No, he didn't. I still think that it was a stray bullet from someone hunting over in those woods."

"Three stray bullets? I don't think so. How about doing me a favor and tell me what was going on between you and Cal? I'm trying to close cases here, and I could use your help. We're pretty sure he tried to blow up

Charlie. We figure he tried to shoot you, but missed and got your nurse."

"Nancy. Her name is Nancy," Bobby told him.

"Right. Nancy. So, we just need to know if he actually ran your boat into that dock on purpose. Whataya say, Bobby? Can you help me out here?"

Bobby smiled. "I'd love nothing better to help you close your case, Sheriff. But, I'm not gonna lie to you. It was an accident. By the way, the insurance investigator agrees. It's been determined that there was a malfunction with the engine."

"So, you're getting an insurance settlement?" Sheriff Berkson questioned.

"I'm getting a whole new boat," Bobby remarked, grinning. "Ain't life grand?"

"For you, maybe. You're one of the few people I know that can fall into a pile of shit and come out smelling like a rose."

Bobby laughed. "I don't know if I'd go that far, but I have been lucky."

"To say the least. I hope you'll change your mind one of these days and tell me what happened."

"I already have. You can close the pages on that chapter, Sheriff. My story's not gonna change."

Sheriff Berkson stood up and started to walk to

211

the front door. He hesitated, turned, and looked back at Bobby. "Did you ever figure out how those snakes got in your house?"

Bobby chuckled. "Wasn't that just the damnedest thing?"

Casey and the Sheriff drove away from Bobby's house and headed back to Hollister. Both were quiet, thinking about the conversation they just had with Bobby.

"He's lying, you know," Casey finally remarked.

"I know."

"Who do you think killed Cal? One of Bobby's goons?"

"I'd think that, except for the fact that Janice Hallman already told me who was at Bobby's when the shooting took place. It agrees with what Bobby said. I don't think she has any reason to lie about it."

"Unless Bobby paid her to cover for them," Casey said.

"Possibly. But I don't think so. She impresses me as a hard-working woman, who takes her job seriously. Plus, she comes from money. There's no reason she would put herself in jeopardy by lying for Bobby."

"So, who else wanted Cal dead?"

212

"With his temper? I'd say a lot of people. We just need to keep looking and hope we get lucky," Sheriff Berkson said.

"I guess," replied Casey. "Have you noticed how many citations Funtelli has written this week?"

Sheriff Berkson grinned. "I guess that chewing out I gave him sunk in. I've never seen him work harder. People are crawling through town at five miles an hour, scared that Funtelli may be hiding behind a billboard."

"Looks like he's finally put that JoJo thing behind him," Casey commented.

"Looks like. You know, Casey, we gotta find him a nice girl. You know anyone?"

"Naw. But, Betsy might. I'll ask her tonight when I get home. We could set Funtelli up with a blind date – or do a couple's thing and go out for dinner. Might be easier that way. You know – to break the ice and all."

"That would be nice," replied the Sheriff, as he pulled into the back of the police station and parked the car.

Chapter Thirty

It had been almost three months since Cal Cuddihey had been murdered. The Hollister Police Department was back to writing traffic tickets, breaking up domestic fights, and leading funeral processions through red lights. The Sheriff welcomed the quiet. He had seen enough death in the past few years to last him a lifetime.

Doc Harris' autopsy report declared the cause of Katie Cuddihey's death as drowning. When the insurance investigator determined that the motor had malfunctioned and caused the accident, Berkson had no choice but to close the case. He did so reluctantly, still believing that Cal Cuddihey had killed her.

Cal Cuddihey's murder remained unsolved. The gun was never recovered and with no evidence as to who did the shooting, the Sheriff figured it would stay unsolved.

Nancy Hallman's shoulder healed nicely, and her doctor told her that with a few more weeks of therapy, it should be as good as new.

Charlie Hoppe was looking forward to getting his new hand. He was dating one of the nurses from the hospital, and he thought marriage might be just around the corner. Sheriff Berkson closed the case on the bombing, citing Cal Cuddihey as the person responsible.

John Luke and Phil Wilson got jobs working construction. They stopped by Bobby's regularly to visit, have a beer, and enjoy a cookout.

Bobby was walking without crutches. He religiously did his exercises and his leg was getting stronger each day. He found that water therapy helped, and he spent a great deal of time in his pool. He wasn't comfortable driving yet, so when he left the house, Sammy drove him. On frequent occasions, Bobby and Sammy would go out drinking at Waxy's Bar. When they'd leave, Bobby would usually bring a woman or two back to the house to party. Sammy, always the faithful husband, would go home to his wife, Alicia.

Officer Simon Funtelli continued to be obsessed with Bobby Johnson. On most days, he would park his car on Harper Lane for ten or fifteen minutes, stare at Bobby's house, and then drive off.

It was a beautiful morning. Although the weather forecast had predicted rain, the sun was shining. It was 72 degrees outside, and the humidity was low. Sheriff Berkson loved days like this and hoped the rain would pass them by. He and his wife, Sarah, had been invited to a cookout, and rain would definitely ruin the outdoor

215

party.

Officer Simon Funtelli was at his desk talking to Deputy Casey George about some local baseball game that had taken place the previous night. The Hollister team had lost by one run, due to a bad call from the home plate umpire, and the fans were pissed. Sheriff Berkson smiled. How nice we're back to arguing about a baseball game, instead of trying to figure out who killed who, he thought.

When the phone rang, the Sheriff glanced over at Officer Tim Carlson, who was on dispatch. Tim answered the call and listened, interrupting the caller a few times to ask a question. When the Sheriff saw the shocked look on Tim's face, he straightened up in his chair. He'd seen that look on Tim's face enough times to know something bad had happened.

"That was Sammy Severson," Tim said, as he hung up the phone. He hesitated for a second. Then, his voice cracking with emotion, said, "He just found Bobby Johnson floating face down in his pool."

"Ah, shit!" Sheriff Berkson exclaimed, as he abruptly stood up, knocking his chair over. He grabbed his hat and headed towards the door.

"Funtelli, with me. Brad, you're with Casey. Let's go."

216

Fifteen minutes later, the Sheriff and his officers were standing at the edge of Bobby's pool, looking at a body floating face down in the water.

"You're sure it's Bobby?" the Sheriff asked Sammy.

"I'm sure. I was gonna jump in and get him. I thought maybe I could do CPR or something, but it was pretty obvious that he was dead. So, I called you guys."

"What time did you find him?"

"About a half-hour ago."

"Did you spend the night here? "

"No. And, as far as I know, he was alone. We went out drinking last night. I dropped him off about one o'clock. He was pretty wasted. I helped him get into bed and I left. That's the last time I saw him, until now," Sammy stated.

"He's naked."

"Not unusual for Bobby. He rarely wore a bathing suit unless there were little kids around."

"What do you think happened?" Sheriff Berkson asked Sammy.

"I'm not sure. Like I said, he was pretty wasted. I figure he woke up and decided to go for a swim. Probably fell, hit his head, and landed in the pool.

Bobby was a good swimmer, so I don't think he'd drown, even if he was drunk. Hell, I don't know, Sheriff. I'm grasping at straws, here."

"Possible, I guess," replied the Sheriff.

"Sheriff," Casey interrupted, "Doc Harris is here."

"Okay. Let's get Bobby out of the water, so the Doc can take a look."

A minute later, Doc Harris walked out of the house and into the pool area. When he saw Bobby's body lying on the cement, he shook his head in disbelief. "Damn, it's Bobby Johnson. The call I got said a body had been found. I wasn't told it was Bobby. They just now pull him out of the water?" he asked Berkson.

"Yep."

"Shit, Sheriff. Bobby had his faults, but I kinda liked the guy."

"I know what you mean. This town won't be the same without Bobby."

Casey smirked. "Damn right it won't. Maybe, now all the crap that's been going on for the past few years will come to an end. I don't know about you two, but it seems to me that every time there's been trouble around here, it had Bobby's name written all over it."

The sheriff gave Casey a dirty look. "How about keeping your thoughts to yourself, Deputy. We don't speak bad of the dead."

"Sorry, Sheriff," Casey said. "But, it's true."

"Well, guess I better go take a look. Sometimes, I hate this job," Doc Harris said and walked over to where Bobby was lying.

Doc Harris took the body temperature to help determine the time of death and noted it in a notebook. He figured Bobby took his last breath between three and five a.m. He'd know more after he filtered in the water temperature, and he could get a more exact reading. He checked Bobby's extremities for cuts or bruises and found none. He lifted Bobby's head off the cement and noted that there was damage to the back of his skull.

"Looks like he was shot," Doc yelled to the Sheriff.

"Damn it all to hell, Doc. Don't be telling me that." The Sheriff walked over to Bobby's body and knelt down. Doc Harris turned Bobby's head towards him, so he could see the entry wound.

"No exit wound?" the Sheriff said.

"Nope. Bullet's most likely still in his head."

"Means a small caliber."

"Most likely," replied Doc Harris. "My bet is a .22. I'll know soon enough, after I get him on the table."

"Casey," the Sheriff yelled. "Start looking for blood. And, a shell casing. Probably from a .22. Check this area

219

first. Call the station and get a few more guys up here. We need to go through the house. Everything's off-limits until we've searched every area. Got it?"

"Got it," Casey replied. "Figures, doesn't it?"

"What's that?" the Sheriff asked.

"Another murder and, even dead, Bobby Johnson manages to be right in the middle of it."

"You're right," the Sheriff concurred. "But, for the last time, Casey. All of Melissa's boys are gone now. My god, that poor woman would roll over in her grave if she saw how they turned out."

"Ya, they're gone," Casey agreed, "Until Tom gets out of prison."

Chapter Thirty-one

It had been three days since Bobby's death. Sheriff Berkson was concentrating on reading a copy of a document that had been delivered to him by Bobby's attorney. He was in Interrogation Room One and had given instructions not to be disturbed.

Sheriff Berkson had been surprised that Bobby had a Will. He didn't consider Bobby the type of person who had the foresight to give much thought to the future. There were two main beneficiaries; his brother Tom and Olivia Frankel. Neither were suspects in Bobby's murder, as Tom was in prison and Olivia was in Texas at the time of the shooting.

Bobby had left Tom his home on Harper Lane and the house that used to belong to Big John. Bobby had bought Big John's house after it went into foreclosure, and was renting it out. Bobby also left Tom a sizable amount of money, some of which was to be used to maintain the two residences, until Tom was released from prison. Bobby also requested that the grandfather clock, which once belonged to his grandpa and, then, his mother, be passed on to Tom.

A lump sum of $250,000.00 was to go to the Cuddihey children, to be used for their college education.

Olivia Frankel was the big winner. Except for a few exceptions, Bobby left her almost all of his monetary assets.

Sheriff Berkson sat up as he read the next paragraph. One million dollars was to be donated to the McKenzie Institute in Kansas City, Missouri. This one-time donation guaranteed that JoJo Kirkham would be allowed to reside there until she was well enough to re-enter society or she died.

"Holy crap," the Sheriff commented out loud. He read the next few sentences and realized that somewhere there was an agreement between Bobby and the Institute. Bobby's attorney probably had a copy of it.

Berkson finished reading the document. Except for a few small donations to charities around Hollister, that was it. He noted the date the document had been signed.

He smiled. Even in death, Bobby continues to surprise me, he thought.

"You find out anything?" Casey asked as the Sheriff walked out of the interrogation room into the office.

"Nothing earth-shattering. Bobby left most everything to Olivia Frankel and his brother, Tom."

"Really? What about Big John? Didn't he leave anything to him?"

'No reason to. He'll never get out of prison. He did request that the funding of Tom's and Big John's prison accounts be continued."

Casey snorted. "That's big of him."

"Are the guys done going through all the stuff from Bobby's house, yet?"

"Just about. They found enough OxyContin to make a crippled man dance. Bobby had a lot of guns, but they're all legal. We haven't found anything so far that's out of the ordinary."

"Well, I don't know about that. I'd like to know why he had so much OxyContin. He must have been getting it from an outside source. There's no way his doctor would have prescribed that much."

"You're right. I'll check that out," Casey said.

"So, we have no idea why someone would want Bobby dead?"

"Not really. I figured when Cal was killed, that was the end of Bobby's problems. Obviously, I was wrong."

"We all thought that, Casey. I think Bobby did, too."

"Did you get Doc's autopsy report, yet?" Casey asked.

"Sure did. Death due to a gunshot wound to the back of the head. It was a .22, by the way. Doc was right about that. He was dead when he hit the water."

"We don't have one suspect. How are we supposed to work a case with absolutely no evidence?"

"We have the bullet," the Sheriff said. "That's where we start."

"I'm out of here," Funtelli interjected.

Sheriff Berkson glanced over at Funtelli's desk. "Where are you going?"

"Out on patrol. Gonna see if I can catch me some bad guys," he said, chuckling.

"Stay safe," Berkson said and turned back to his conversation with Casey.

Funtelli drove out of Hollister on Hwy. 76, and turned onto Lake Shore Drive. He drove up the hilly road to the same spot where he had parked a few months ago. He exited his squad car and stretched. He walked to the edge of the cliff and looked down at the water. God, I love this place, he thought. I love the hills and valleys, the rivers and lakes. I'm gonna miss it so much.

He reached into his pocket and pulled out a gun. It was so small that it easily fit into the palm of his hand. He smiled as he flung it into the water below. He watched until he saw the small splash it made, as it hit the beautiful blue water of Lake Taneycomo.

Funtelli sat on the edge of the cliff, finally feeling at peace. He looked up at the blue sky and smiled.

There were no clouds today.

Epilogue

It's been a year since Bobby Johnson was laid to rest. He's buried next to his mother, Melissa, on a hill overlooking Lake Taneycomo. There are no flowers on his grave, and the grass has turned brown in the dry, summer heat.

Bobby's mobile home is empty. The furniture is covered with large white sheets, to protect it from dust. His attorney, who is also the executor of his estate, hired a lawn service to maintain the outside of the house. They rarely show up and the yard is overgrown with weeds.

The Olympic-sized pool is empty and the bottom is covered with brown, rotting leaves that fell during the late fall season.

Having found access through a small hole in the kitchen, a family of mice now roams from room to room inside Bobby's old house. They have multiplied considerably, as mice do, and the once expensive furniture is now being inhabited by these little, nasty, germ-ridden critters.

Bobby's plane has been sold, as have his multiple vehicles. The money was deposited into an account, which his attorney refers to as The Maintenance Money Account. The money is almost gone, having been used to fund several vacations for himself and his family.

Officer Funtelli resigned from his job and moved out west. Although he said he'd stay in touch, no one has heard from him since he left Hollister.

Deputy Casey George and his wife, Betsy, are expecting their second child in February. After numerous failures, Betsy finally gave up trying to make Mrs. Berkson's meatloaf recipe.

A few months after Bobby's death, Sheriff Berkson drove by Bobby's old home. As he glanced over at the house, he noticed that the mailbox door was open. He pulled up to the box, removed what he assumed was junk mail, closed the door, and drove away.

Since that day, a postcard found between some flyers in that mail, rests on Sheriff Berkson's desk. It is the first thing he sees when he comes to work in the morning and the last thing before he leaves at night.

On one side, of the postcard, there is a picture of a boat anchored in a beautiful blue lagoon. On the other side, next to Bobby's address, is scrawled this message.

Bobby,

Need any more trash taken out? My boat needs repairs and I need $$$.

BTW-I named her THE MELISSA J.

Hook

Floating Face Down - - - - - - - Susan L. Pare'

About the Author

I was born in Idaho in 1939. My father's job demanded that we frequently move so, by the age of ten, I had lived in Idaho, Montana, Colorado, Michigan, and finally Wisconsin.

I am the proud mother of three wonderful sons and two fantastic grandsons. I have no plans to acquire another husband, as they are just too much work.

For most of my life, I worked as an accountant. Two years before I retired, I did a complete switch in careers and managed two Curves fitness facilities in Illinois. I retired in 2002 and moved to Branson, MO. In 2012, I moved to Indiana to be closer to my family and have resided in Highland since then.

I enjoy a good laugh and figure it's my sense of humor that has kept me going when times were tough. Reading has always been one of my passions and I still read a couple of books a week.

Most of my life, I have written poems for amusement. In 2014, I wrote my first book, *Blueberries and Bears and My Brother's Shoes*, a book about growing up in the forties and fifties. After I self-published it and gave it to friends and family to read, they encouraged me to get serious about my writing.

Crossing Sydney was my first novel and it was

published in July 2015. It has received outstanding reviews.

Don't Smother Your Mother was my second book, and I had fun writing it. Although it's a mystery, I threw humor into it and made it an easy-to-read whodunit. *A Bad Week in Hollister* picks up where *Don't Smother Your Mother* leaves off, with another mystery for Sheriff "Cowboy" Berkson to solve.

Let's Play Autopsy takes place in Kalispell, Montana. The persons and places are fictitious, although at one time in my life I did live on 3rd Avenue East. Writing this book definitely took me back to some of my childhood memories. The house I lived in is still standing, although it looks a little worn. But, then, so do I. I guess we could all use a new coat of paint now and then.

Floating Face Down, is the third and final book in the Sheriff "Cowboy" Berkson series. I wavered a lot about the ending, as I knew it meant the end of writing about some of my favorite characters. However, I figured there are a lot of other people roaming around in my head that can wind up in a book. So, I said goodbye to Cowboy and his men.

I never thought that, at the age of 76, I would become an author. I have set a goal for myself to write ten books before I die. I guess I better stick with it because you just never know.

I certainly am enjoying my retirement knowing, when I get up each morning, I have something to look forward to. You can find out more about me and my books at www.susanlpare.com. Please visit me there and feel free to send me your comments.

Floating Face Down - - - - - - - Susan L. Pare'